*Nick had a bad feeling…
a very bad feeling.*

He wasn't sure if it was because of the disturbing dream he'd just suffered or because of the news he'd just received. But as his gaze met Alyssa's, he suddenly realized a connection he hadn't made before.

Men in Cherokee Corners were being stabbed to death, and for the past month Alyssa Whitefeather had been having visions of herself stabbing a man to death. Was there a connection? Was she tapped into some sort of energy she didn't even realize or understand?

There was no time to question the issue with her now, but he realized that no matter how painful it was for her, no matter how uncomfortable the visions made her, and despite his desire to protect her, they were going to have to explore the depths of her psychic abilities.

He was beginning to think that perhaps Alyssa's mind might hold the only key that would lead to their killer.

Dear Reader,

Once again, Silhouette Intimate Moments has a month's worth of fabulous reading for you. Start by picking up *Wanted,* the second in Ruth Langan's suspenseful DEVIL'S COVE miniseries. This small town is full of secrets, and this top-selling author knows how to keep readers turning the pages.

We have more terrific miniseries. Kathleen Creighton continues STARRS OF THE WEST with *An Order of Protection,* featuring a protective hero every reader will want to have on her side. In *Joint Forces,* Catherine Mann continues WINGMEN WARRIORS with Tag's long-awaited story. Seems Tag and his wife are also awaiting something: the unexpected arrival of another child. Carla Cassidy takes us back to CHEROKEE CORNERS in *Manhunt.* There's a serial killer on the loose, and only the heroine's visions can help catch him—but will she be in time to save the hero? *Against the Wall* is the next SPECIAL OPS title from Lyn Stone, a welcome addition to the line when she's not also writing for Harlequin Historicals. Finally, you knew her as Anne Avery, also in Harlequin Historicals, but now she's Anne Woodard, and in *Dead Aim* she proves she knows just what contemporary readers want.

Enjoy them all—and come back next month, when Silhouette Intimate Moments brings you even more of the best and most exciting romance reading around.

Yours,

Leslie J. Wainger
Executive Editor

Please address questions and book requests to:
Silhouette Reader Service
U.S.: 3010 Walden Ave., P.O. Box 1325, Buffalo, NY 14269
Canadian: P.O. Box 609, Fort Erie, Ont. L2A 5X3

Manhunt
CARLA CASSIDY

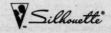

INTIMATE MOMENTS™

Published by Silhouette Books

America's Publisher of Contemporary Romance

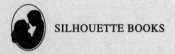 **SILHOUETTE BOOKS**

ISBN 0-373-27364-9

MANHUNT

This edition published by arrangement with Harlequin Books S.A.

® and TM are trademarks of Harlequin Books S.A., used under license.
Trademarks indicated with ® are registered in the United States Patent
and Trademark Office, the Canadian Trade Marks Office and in other
countries.

Visit Silhouette Books at www.eHarlequin.com

Printed in U.S.A.

Books by Carla Cassidy

Silhouette Intimate Moments

One of the Good Guys #531
Try To Remember #560
Fugitive Father #604
Behind Closed Doors #778
†*Reluctant Wife* #850
†*Reluctant Dad* #856
‡*Her Counterfeit Husband* #885
‡*Code Name: Cowboy* #902
‡*Rodeo Dad* #934
In a Heartbeat #1005
‡*Imminent Danger* #1018
**Strangers When We Married* #1046
***Man on a Mission* #1077
Born of Passion #1094
***Once Forbidden...* #1115
***To Wed and Protect* #1126
***Out of Exile* #1149
Secrets of a Pregnant Princess #1166
‡‡*Last Seen...* #1233
‡‡*Dead Certain* #1250
‡‡*Trace Evidence* #1261
‡‡*Manhunt* #1294

The Coltons

Pregnant in Prosperino

Lone Star Country Club

Promised to a Sheik

Silhouette Books

Shadows 1993
"Devil and the Deep Blue Sea"

Silhouette Yours Truly

Pop Goes the Question

†*Sisters*
‡*Mustang, Montana*
***The Delaney Heirs*
‡‡*Cherokee Corners*
**The Baker Brood*
††*The Pregnancy Test*

Silhouette Romance

Patchwork Family #818
Whatever Alex Wants... #856
Fire and Spice #884
Homespun Hearts #905
Golden Girl #924
Something New #942
Pixie Dust #958
The Littlest Matchmaker #978
The Marriage Scheme #996
Anything for Danny #1048
**Deputy Daddy* #1141
**Mom in the Making* #1147
**An Impromptu Proposal* #1152
**Daddy on the Run* #1158
Pregnant with His Child... #1259
Will You Give My Mommy a Baby? #1315
‡*Wife for a Week* #1400
The Princess's White Knight #1415
Waiting for the Wedding #1426
Just One Kiss #1496
Lost in His Arms #1514
An Officer and a Princess #1522
More Than Meets the Eye #1602
††*What If I'm Pregnant...?* #1644
††*If the Stick Turns Pink...* #1645
A Gift from the Past #1669
Rules of Engagement #1702

Silhouette Desire

A Fleeting Moment #784
Under the Boardwalk #882

Silhouette Shadows

Swamp Secrets #4
Heart of the Beast #11
Silent Screams #25
Mystery Child #61

The Loop

Getting It Right: Jessica

CARLA CASSIDY

is an award-winning author who has written over fifty books for Silhouette. In 1995, she won Best Silhouette Romance from *Romantic Times* for *Anything for Danny*. In 1998, she also won a Career Achievement Award for Best Innovative Series from *Romantic Times*.

Carla believes the only thing better than curling up with a good book to read is sitting down at the computer with a good story to write. She's looking forward to writing many more books and bringing hours of pleasure to readers.

Chapter 1

He didn't want to be here, but his choices had been limited. Take a desk job, get out of town and into the field or look for a new job. The first and third options were unthinkable so <u>Nick Mead</u> had taken the second option.

He now slowed his speed and turned down the radio playing oldies as he realized he had to be approaching the small Podunk town where he would head up a task force looking for a killer.

Tightening his hands on the steering wheel, he thought of another killer, a madman who had destroyed his life and tormented him for the past three years.

He called himself <u>Murphy</u>, but most of the men in the bureau called him <u>NOP</u>…an acronym that stood for Nick's Own Psycho.

After three years of hunting, hating and hungering for revenge, Nick, at times, felt as psycho as the man he sought.

He knew that was one of the reasons his supervisor had sent him out into the middle of nowhere. The big guys in the bureau thought Nick was on the edge, obsessed with a single case and of course, they were right on both counts.

He slowed down even more as he approached a sign that welcomed him to Cherokee Corners, Oklahoma. Officially he and his two-man team weren't expected until the next day, but Nick had decided to arrive early and get a feel for the town and its people.

The main area of town was built on a charming center square. The mayor's office and the post office were in the center, surrounded by a lush parklike setting. It took him only moments to recognize the town as a diverse mix of Native Americans and Caucasians.

Although Nick had spent the last three and a half years working out of the Tulsa office, he knew very little about Native Americans and their culture. Before Tulsa he'd worked for seven years in Chicago. He was well versed in Latino tradition, Italian culture and Irish pride, but he knew next to nothing about Indian life.

Too big to be a town, too small to be called a city, Cherokee Corners seemed to exist somewhere in between. The previous chief of police, <u>Thomas James</u>, had been a man of vision. Nick knew he'd imple-

mented a small crime lab and had several crime scene
investigators working for the department.

Nick also knew there were three places in a town
to learn the pulse of the people who lived there—the
local watering hole, the barbershop and the café or
diner.

He didn't want a drink, didn't need a haircut, but
his stomach had been growling enough to let him
know it was lunchtime.

There were three cafés at various places around the
center square. He chose the one that looked the bus-
iest.

A cacophony of sounds and scents greeted him as
he walked through the door. The overriding odor was
one of frying hamburgers and onions, but beneath that
pungent scent was the faint fragrance of cooked ap-
ples and baking bread.

The place was packed. Clinking silverware, chatter
and laughter and a cook calling "order up" all created the chorus that sang of a successful establishment.

A big older woman with blond hair in a sort of
beehive concoction greeted him from behind the cash
register. "Tables and booths are all full, handsome,
but if you don't mind being a counter fly there's a
stool open at the end."

He'd noticed that the name of the place was Ruby's
Café and had a feeling the woman was none other
than Ruby herself. "Thanks," he said and smiled. "I
guess being a counter fly is better than being a bar-
fly."

She grinned, her blue-shadowed eyes sparkling in amusement. "Ah, not only are you handsome as sin, but you have a sense of humor, too. If I were two decades younger I'd have you for lunch."

He winked at her. "If I were two decades older...I'd let you."

She was still laughing as he slid onto the empty stool at the end of the counter. He opened his menu, quickly made his selection, then leaned back in the stool and tuned into the bits and pieces of conversations that floated in the air around him.

A table of farmer types were complaining about the weather and predicting a long rough winter. Two women at another nearby table were discussing the trauma of potty training, and the two men closest to him at the counter were discussing the latest nosedive on Wall Street.

The atmosphere in Ruby's was one of peaceful coexistence, a comfortableness among the patrons and a sense of community as people departed and arrived and waves and smiles were exchanged.

"Sorry you had to wait," a young waitress said as she stopped before him, order pad at the ready.

"No problem. Just a burger and fries," Nick said. "And a glass of milk."

By the time his order had arrived, some of the lunch crowd had dispersed and only Nick and two other men remained at the counter.

Nick ate quickly then lingered over a cup of coffee and a piece of apple pie.

"How's that pie?" The big-haired blonde moved

from behind the cash register to stand on the opposite side of the counter in front of Nick.

"Best I've ever had," he replied truthfully.

"Just passing through or sticking around?" she asked with open curiosity. "By the way, I'm Ruby, owner of this fine establishment." She stuck out a meaty hand with long, scarlet fingernails.

"Nick Mead. Nice to meet you and I think I'm sticking around for a while."

"Good. This town could use a little more eye candy when it comes to the male population."

"Why, I do believe you're flirting with me, Ms. Ruby."

She laughed and nodded her head, blond curls bobbing on plump shoulders. "I come by it naturally."

She leaned over the counter and winked at him conspiratorially. "My great-grandma owned and ran the first brothel in these here parts. I come from a long line of flirts and lovers." She stepped back from the counter and patted her big belly. "Unfortunately, I like my food better than I like most men."

He laughed, then sobered. "Maybe you can help me, Ruby. I plan on hanging around town for a while, but I need a place to stay. I pulled up the Cherokee Corners home page on the Internet and noticed there were several options. Maybe you can direct me someplace?" Although the agency always made arrangements for the men they sent out in the field, Nick usually opted to make his own. Besides, the locals always knew which places were good and which were not so great.

Ruby frowned. "No hotels in town and the only motel is out by the highway. I suppose the sheets are clean enough but I wouldn't go swimming in that swamp water they call a pool. If you want to be treated well and like a little extra TLC, there's the Redbud Bed-and-Breakfast across the square. If you decide to go there, tell Alyssa I sent you."

"Alyssa?"

"Alyssa Whitefeather. She owns the place, including the ice-cream parlor that's the bottom floor."

"Thanks, Ruby."

"No problem...and don't be a stranger." She moved back to the cash register to take care of a departing diner.

As Nick finished up his coffee and pie, he thought about what to do for accommodations. Cherokee Corners was a town that thrived on the tourist trade and the Web page had listed half a dozen places for overnight accommodations.

He had no idea how long he would be in Cherokee Corners. It could be a week or two, it could be a month or more. Certainly the amenities of a bed-and-breakfast sounded far more appealing than a motel room, especially if his stay would end up being a prolonged one.

Besides, he hadn't been in a motel room for almost three years. As he walked from Ruby's to his car, his mind flashed visions of the last time he'd been in a motel room.

It had been the somber and sympathetic faces of his co-workers that had told him it was bad. They'd tried to keep him out, to talk him into not going inside the room, but he'd needed to see.

He still remembered the painting that had hung on the wall directly above the bed. At first he'd thought it was some sort of weird abstraction of sorts. It took him a moment to realize it had once been a serene landscape before blood had splattered it and run in rivulets down the canvas.

He hadn't wanted to look at the bed, but knew he had to…he had to see with his own eyes that Murphy had followed him from Chicago to Tulsa, that Murphy had extracted a price of revenge that was beyond comprehension.

She lay there, blond hair splayed like sunshine on what had been a burnt gold bedspread. That's what he'd called her…his sunshine. Dorrie…his sunshine, his wife of five years.

The last time he'd seen her had been that morning as they'd shared breakfast. It had been over scrambled eggs and wheat toast that they'd decided it was time to try to start a family. With her blue eyes shining brightly, she'd told him she wanted his baby.

Now she lay sprawled on the bed, naked and with a garish grinlike wound where her throat had been slashed from ear to ear. On her chest, a postmortem wound in the shape of a capital M—Murphy's signature.

He slid behind the steering wheel of his car and consciously shoved the painful images out of his mind. He couldn't think about that now. He couldn't let thoughts of Murphy screw up the case he was about to take on. He had a murderer to find right here in Cherokee Corners.

But, eventually he'd find Murphy. His fingers curled painfully tight around the steering wheel as cold, barely controlled rage filled him. Eventually the son of a bitch would pay in the worst kind of way for taking Dorrie's life.

"If you take care of restocking the napkins, I'll refresh the toppings," Alyssa said to Mary, the young, blond-haired woman who helped her out through the summers at the ice-cream parlor that comprised the bottom floor of the Redbud Bed-and-Breakfast.

"Okay," Mary agreed good-naturedly.

Alyssa smiled warmly at the woman. She'd been a blessing in the past couple of months. Mary had not only pitched in and worked more hours than usual, but had supported Alyssa emotionally through dark days, when it had seemed that every evil spirit in the world had tormented the people Alyssa loved.

Things had calmed down for the moment, at least for the James family, the people Alyssa claimed as her own. Alyssa's aunt Rita, who had been kidnapped two months ago had been returned safe and sound to her family.

It had been a town scandal of massive proportions when it was discovered that Jacob Kincaid, the wealthy, respected owner of one of the banks in town, had sneaked into Alyssa's aunt and uncle's home, hit her uncle Thomas over the head and kidnapped Rita.

He'd held her in his basement for weeks while the rest of the family had gone crazy trying to find her.

It was only through the police work of Alyssa's three cousins, <u>Savannah, Breanna and Clay</u>, that Rita had been found and Jacob Kincaid arrested. It was later discovered that there had been two women before Aunt Rita, women who had not been rescued but who Jacob had killed.

The silver lining, if there could be one, was that through the course of the investigation, her cousins had all discovered love as they searched for their missing mother.

Alyssa should be feeling the reflecting, warm happiness of the people she loved, but instead she was exhausted, reeling from the latest bout of visions she'd been suffering…visions of bloody and violent death.

It didn't help that a serial killer was loose in the town. In Alyssa's mind this would always be the summer of fear…first because of her aunt Rita's kidnapping and now because of the heinous murders taking place in Cherokee Corners.

"I'll bet the whole town turns out next week for <u>Clay and Tamara</u>'s wedding," Mary said as she busily filled the napkin holders.

Alyssa smiled, grateful for any topic that would momentarily take her mind off her worries. "I still can't believe that stubborn cousin of mine agreed to be married in a traditional Cherokee ceremony."

"It doesn't surprise me. He'd do anything for Tamara. There is only one thing better than the love of a good woman,'' Mary began.

''And that's the love of a good man.'' Alyssa laughed as they both chorused the words.

She got busy refilling the bins that contained nuts, multicolored candy sprinkles, chocolate chips and all the goodies kids liked to use to top off their ice-cream cones.

She wouldn't mind having the love of a good man in her life, but that wasn't likely to happen as long as she lived here in Cherokee Corners. Too many of the eligible bachelors in town were either frightened by her or thought her crazy.

Besides, she didn't have time for romance. Between running the bed-and-breakfast and the ice-cream parlor, she barely had time to breathe. Things were especially busy this time of year, when the late-August heat made the thought of a banana split or a sundae particularly attractive and tourists filled the town.

Things would slow down in a couple of weeks when school began again. The kids of the town would disappear back into classrooms and the tourists would return home until next summer.

''I'll be right back,'' Alyssa said. ''I've got to get more sprinkles from the storeroom.''

''While you're doing that I'll make sure all the tables and chairs are clean,'' Mary replied.

Alyssa smiled her thanks, then entered the storeroom and began the hunt for the candied sprinkles amid the other stock. As she searched she heard the tinkling bell over the ice-cream-parlor door announce the arrival of the first customer of the day.

"Good afternoon." Mary's voice rang out with her usual cheerfulness.

"Good afternoon to you, too." The deep, smooth male voice was unfamiliar to Alyssa.

"What can I get for you? Our special this week is our Brownie Delight for only ninety-nine cents," Mary said as Alyssa located the plastic jug of candy sprinkles.

"Actually, I'm not here for ice cream. My name is Nick Mead and I just arrived in town. Ruby from the café across the square sent me over here. I need a room."

At that moment Alyssa stepped out of the storeroom and had her first look at the man inquiring about a room. Shock held her rooted in place. A rushing wind resounded in her ears as the plastic jug of candy slipped from her fingers and hit the floor.

"We have no rooms available." She heard the voice above the roar of the wind and recognized it as her own.

"Alyssa...remember, the <u>Carlsons</u> checked out late last night. The blue room is available," Mary said.

Words of protest refused to rise to Alyssa's lips as Nick Mead's intense blue eyes gazed at her curiously.

All she knew was an incredible need to escape from his gaze, from his very presence. "You take care of it, Mary." With the roar of dangerous winds still deafening her, Alyssa left the jug of sprinkles lying where it had fallen and escaped through the door that led to her private living quarters.

She went directly to the sofa and sank down, afraid her trembling legs wouldn't hold her up a moment longer. The vision. She grabbed a strand of her long dark hair and worried it between two fingers, trying to shove away the thought of the recurring vision she'd been having for the past month or so.

She'd suffered with visions all her life but none had been as vivid, as disturbing as the one that had recently haunted her, the one that had included a man who looked exactly like the one who had just walked into her establishment.

She didn't know how long she sat there, lost in a haze of stunned shock, when a light tap on her door pulled her from her nightmarish reverie.

"Come in," she called.

The door opened and Mary peeked her head in, concern wrinkling her forehead. "Are you okay?"

For a split second Alyssa wanted to tell Mary exactly what tormented her, but she'd told nobody about the terrifying, horrible visions she'd been experiencing. She now tried to shove those images aside and focus on her friend.

She forced a smile to her lips. "I'm fine. I don't know what happened in there. I was suddenly very light-headed and dizzy."

"Have you eaten anything at all today?" Mary sighed audibly as Alyssa shook her head. "I swear, Alyssa, you're up before dawn every morning cooking breakfast to take care of your guests, but you never take the time to take care of yourself.''

"I'll fix something now," Alyssa said. "I'm just giving myself a minute or two to get my feet back under me again."

"Take your time. I've got everything under control," Mary assured her. "I got Mr. Mead settled in the blue room. I don't know if you noticed or not before you got all wobbly, but that man is definitely lust-after material." Mary winked, wiggled her fingers in a goodbye gesture, then closed the door and left Alyssa alone.

Alyssa closed her eyes and drew a deep breath in an attempt to steady herself. She still felt cold and shaky and knew it was the residual effects of experiencing complete and utter shock.

Nick Mead. She now knew his name. Mary had said he was "lust-after material" but she didn't have to tell Alyssa that. Although she was a virtual stranger to Nick Mead, he was intimately familiar to her.

For the last month she'd had visions of making love to a stranger, a handsome man with dark hair and ice-blue eyes. She knew exactly how his lips made demands when he kissed, knew the white-hot heat his caressing fingers could evoke. She knew the rhythm of his hips against her own as they made hot, frantic love.

She knew all this and yet she hadn't known his name until now, had never met him before today. For the past month she'd been haunted by visions of the handsome Nick Mead, visions that came from some unidentifiable force, visions that almost invariably came true.

She had no idea what force had brought him here to Cherokee Corners, but she didn't want him here. She didn't want him in town and she certainly didn't want him under her roof. Danger...her brain screamed. His appearance here, the reality of him, made her head ache with dread.

But he was here...in Cherokee Corners, a guest in her bed-and-breakfast. Maybe he would only stay the night then be gone with the morning dawn.

Struggling up to her feet, a momentary wave of hope winged through her at this thought. If he left first thing in the morning, then it was quite possible she wouldn't see him or talk to him again and maybe her terrible visions of him would cease.

An icy chill once again clutched her as she thought of the visions that had haunted her for the past month. The visions of making love to him wasn't what frightened her, but each time, the vision ended with her stabbing him in the chest...stabbing him over and over again.

Chapter 2

As Nick unpacked his suitcase and hung his clothes in the armoire and dresser in the charming room decorated in various shades of blue, his thoughts weren't on his surroundings but rather on the woman he'd seen briefly downstairs.

The antithesis of Dorrie, who had been sunshine and light, Alyssa Whitefeather had seemed like a woman cloaked in darkness.

Long, black hair had spilled down over her shoulders and her skin tones had been dusky, the cinnamon tones of Native American blood. High cheekbones had further attested to her heritage. Her eyes, dark blue, had been a shock, startling with their unexpected hue.

She'd been wearing a shapeless light blue sundress but it had been easy to tell that beneath the flowing material she was thin, but not without feminine curves.

As he took his toiletries into the adjoining bathroom, he couldn't help but contemplate the expression that had taken over her lovely features in the instant she'd gazed at him.

Shock…stunned disbelief…it was as if she'd seen a ghost when she'd looked at him.

He stacked his personal items on the sink countertop. Shaving cream, razor, cologne, deodorant and a large bottle of aspirin marked the territory as his own for the duration of his stay, a stay he'd told Mary would be indefinite.

Maybe he looked like an old boyfriend who'd dumped her, or a cheating ex-husband. He knew for sure he'd never seen her before in his life. Nick had a knack for remembering faces. He wasn't always great with names, but faces he never forgot and he was positive he'd never seen Alyssa Whitefeather before in his life.

He dismissed her from his mind as he returned to the bedroom and finished unpacking his clothes. When he'd emptied his suitcase, he turned to the briefcase. He walked over to a small table covered with a blue gingham tablecloth that sat in the corner with a window on either side.

He moved the vase filled with fresh-cut flowers from the center of the table to the top of the dresser, then set his briefcase on the table and opened it.

Inside were copies of files from the Cherokee Corners Police Department…the reasons he and his team had been requested to come to town. His two-man team would arrive tomorrow, the date when the chief of police, Glen Cleberg, was expecting them.

A serial killer was terrorizing Cherokee Corners, and after four murders, Chief Cleburg had finally called the FBI for help.

As a criminal profiler, Nick had seen more than his share of evil. As a man he'd tasted the horror of evil in his personal life. That particular horror had begun to fade with the passing of time.

Grief over Dorrie's ugly death didn't fill his every waking hour as it had in the days and weeks after her murder, but the rage had never left him.

He refused to allow the grief or rage to take hold of him now. He had a job to do here, and in order to do it to the best of his ability he had to remain un-emotional and detached. In order to be successful he had to attempt to immerse himself in the life, the mind and the very evil of the murderer at work in this place.

One of the reasons Nick had decided to come a day earlier than his team was because he knew how important it was to get a feel for the town, for the people where a serial killer was at work. He liked giving himself a little time to soak up the local ambience before he dived into the task-force work.

With this thought in mind he opened the first file folder. He'd already read them all half a dozen times, but he'd continue to reread them until he had every fact, every piece of evidence and every nuance of the crimes completely memorized.

If his stomach hadn't started protesting the absence

of food, he probably would have sat at the small table in the corner of the room halfway through the night.

When he could no longer ignore the emptiness and rumbling, he looked at his wristwatch, surprised to realize it was almost seven o'clock.

As Mary had led him to his room, she'd given him a quick rundown on the bed-and-breakfast routine. Breakfast was served in the main dining room between the hours of six and nine in the morning.

The front door was locked at ten o'clock but the guests were given a key to the back door, where they could come and go as they pleased no matter what the hour.

The amenities that came with the room, not counting breakfast itself, were fresh flowers in the room daily, fresh-squeezed lemonade, sun tea and cookies every afternoon on the veranda and turndown service at night if requested.

At the moment Nick wasn't interested in anything other than dinner. The burger he'd had at noon had been great, so he decided Ruby's was the place for dinner, as well.

He left the bed-and-breakfast by the back door and entered an alley that ran along the back of all the establishments on the street. The August heat created a rather unpleasant odor in the alley as he passed several trash bins that likely contained spoiled food.

He followed the alley around the square, noting entrances and exits as he walked. All four victims of the killer had been left at various points in the center square. The alley made an easy, accessible escape route for the killer.

When he reached the back of Ruby's restaurant, he walked around the side of the building, from the alley to the front sidewalk and the door.

Ruby still stood at the cash register and her broad face beamed when he walked through the door. "Ah, a repeat customer. That's a good sign," she said.

He grinned. "It was a piece of great apple pie and I'm hoping you offer something equally as appetizing for your dinner meals."

"You look like a steak man. We've got a great sirloin meal in the evenings. And you're in luck, most of the dinner crowd has thinned out, so you can have your choice of a table or a booth."

Nick quickly perused the place. "A table," he said. The tables were in the center of the room.

"You got it." Ruby left the register and grabbed a menu from a stack, then led him to a small table for two. "This all right?"

"Perfect." He accepted the menu from her and smiled his thanks.

"How about a cup of coffee to start you off?"

"Sounds great."

Moments later Nick sat at the table alone, sipping his coffee while he waited for his steak dinner to arrive. If the cops in the town were as friendly as the other folks, it would make Nick's time here much more pleasant.

A young couple sat next to him and he couldn't help but overhear the argument they were engaged in.

"You promised me no more evening meetings until after the killer is caught," the young woman said, her voice emotional.

"I know, honey, but tonight can't be helped. It was the only time Mr. <u>Maynard</u> could meet with us."

Nick tuned out the conversation, but it intrigued him nevertheless. It was the first time he'd heard anyone mention the killer that plagued the town.

He could understand the fear of the women in town...fear for their male friends, boyfriends or husbands. So far all the victims had been males between the ages of thirty and forty. They'd been stabbed to death and left naked in a public area around the center square.

The steak was grilled to perfection and the baked potato was just the way he liked it, smothered in real butter and sour cream.

As he ate, he found himself wondering how well he and his team would be greeted by the local law enforcement. Even though it had been the Cherokee Corners chief of police that had requested their help, that didn't mean the locals would be particularly pleased to have outsiders working the case.

The bad blood between FBI men and city officers had become almost mythical in the passing of years. Usually, everyone managed to work together without ego or territorial battles in order to solve a particular crime...usually, but not always.

It would be interesting to see what kind of welcome they'd receive here in Cherokee Corners. Hopefully, it would be a good one and he wouldn't have to worry about internal politics or other such nonsense. All he wanted to do was solve this particular case and return to Tulsa and the hunt for the killer named Murphy who had stolen his life.

He was lingering over coffee, when Ruby approached him and motioned to the chair opposite his. ''Mind if I join you for a minute?''

''Not at all,'' he replied, grateful for a break from his own thoughts.

''Steak okay?''

''Perfect. I think this is going to be my favorite place to eat while I'm in town.''

Ruby nodded and grinned. ''Best place in town… although I might be a slight bit prejudiced. Did you get settled in at the Redbud Bed-and-Breakfast?''

''I did, and thanks for the recommendation.''

Ruby nodded again, but the smile that had decorated her face fell away. ''Cherokee Corners is a nice town. We got a good bunch of people here, a nice mix of Native Americans and white folks. We accept each other and live together in peace.''

Nick wondered where she was going with this particular conversation, but he kept silent as she continued. ''Folks help out other folks here. We try to take care of each other, and that's why I thought I'd better warn you. We got trouble in this town right now and it's best if you don't find yourself walking the square after dark.''

''You're talking about the Shameless Slasher,'' he said.

She looked at him in surprise. ''Yeah, that's what

the newspaper calls him. Sick animal is more like it. I like you, Nick. I don't want to see you hurt while you're in Cherokee Corners. I just thought you needed to know about the danger of men going out after dark.''

He smiled, touched by the woman's caring. ''Actually, the killings are what brought me here. I'm an FBI agent and I've been assigned to the case.''

''Well, I'll be damned,'' Ruby exclaimed. ''Here I've been sitting with an official G-man and didn't even know it. I thought you boys always wore suits.''

Nick laughed. ''In this kind of heat? Not this G-man, at least not until I'm officially on duty, and that isn't until tomorrow.''

Ruby leaned toward him, bringing with her a powerful scent of perfume. ''Are you packing?''

''Always,'' he said, thinking of the ankle holster that fit snug against the skin beneath his jeans.

''Then I guess I won't worry about you.''

''Hopefully when I finish my work here, you won't have to worry about anyone,'' Nick replied.

A few minutes later he left the café. Night had just begun to fall, shadows usurping the light in the alley first. He didn't take the alley, but rather walked around the square back to the ice-cream parlor.

All he needed to finish off the good steak meal was a strawberry sundae and maybe a little chat with the intriguing Alyssa Whitefeather.

It was quarter until nine when he walked through the door that he'd first entered earlier in the day.

There were several people seated at the round tables, finishing up sodas and ice-cream treats.

Alyssa stood behind the counter and her eyes darkened as she saw him enter. If he didn't know better, he would guess that it was a visceral dislike that sparked from her eyes. But how was that possible? She didn't know anything about him.

He walked up to the counter and scooted onto a stool and offered her a friendly smile. It was not returned. "What can I get for you, Mr. Mead?"

"How about a strawberry sundae, and please, make it Nick, since I'm going to be staying here for a while."

She made no comment, but turned her back and began to prepare his ice cream. Her long, dark hair was now pulled back at the nape of her neck, caught and held there by a light blue barrette. Her movements were efficient, but graceful at the same time.

From the back she was quite pleasant to look at, but when she turned to face him, her eyes were fathomless and unfriendly. She set the ice-cream treat in front of him then started to walk away.

"Whom do I talk to about turndown service?" he asked.

She stopped walking and turned back to look at him. She was quite pretty. Her skin appeared flawless, her bone structure delicate, and her lips were full but pressed tightly together at the moment. "That would be me," she said.

"Great, then I'd like the service."

"Fine." Once again she started to move away and once again he stopped her by speaking to her.

"Are you always this friendly with guests or is it just me you don't particularly like?"

Her cheeks took on a little more color as she drew a deep breath. "It has nothing to do with liking or disliking you. Mr. Mead, I don't know what brought you to Cherokee Corners, but you should leave."

The words tumbled from her as if she was unable to help herself. "You shouldn't be here in this town and you shouldn't be staying in my bed-and-breakfast."

Nick wondered if she didn't know exactly who he was and why he was here. Was it possible she knew something about the murders? "Lady, what in the hell are you talking about?"

Alyssa stared at him, horrified by what she'd said and even more horrified as she realized he expected an explanation from her.

She couldn't tell him about her visions, he'd think she was some kind of nut. "I just think you should know there is a murderer loose in Cherokee Corners and it isn't safe for you to be here. It isn't safe for any men alone to be in town." There, that didn't sound too crazy, she thought.

"I know all about the Shameless Slasher." He picked up his spoon and dipped it into the strawberry-covered ice cream. "That's why I'm here."

Alyssa stared at him in surprise. On some level she felt herself examining his sinfully handsome good looks, looking for something that would tell her he was not the man she'd been having the horrible visions about.

His dark hair was clipped neatly, although it had just enough wave to soften the cut. He had a Roman nose and below that a wide mouth with sensual lips. But it was his eyes that made him so striking, those intense blue eyes against the foil of his dark hair and tanned face. Unlike the blue of her eyes, which was dark, more a midnight kind of blue, his were the color of a cloudless summer sky.

The same man. There was absolutely, positively no doubt in her mind that he was the same man who had occupied center stage in her latest bout of visions.

"What do you mean that's why you're here?" She finally responded to his words.

"I'm an FBI agent, Alyssa," he said. "Beginning tomorrow, two other agents will be working with me and your police department to find the killer."

An FBI agent. Alyssa reeled with this new knowledge. Why had her visions shown her killing an FBI agent who had come to town to offer his expertise in catching the killer?

"Eat your ice cream before it melts," she said absently, then turned to Tina, the teenage girl who helped her out in the evenings. "I'll be right back."

Tina nodded and Alyssa hurried through a door that led to the upstairs so she could attend to the turndown service he'd requested.

She took the stairs that led to the four bedrooms on the second level. She could tell that in three of them the occupants had already gone into their rooms for the night. Doorknob hangers read, Do Not Disturb.

The fourth room, what they referred to as the blue bedroom, was Alyssa's favorite. The furniture was cherrywood antiques in beautiful condition. The double bed was covered with a light blue gingham print and lace-eyelet spread. Light blue curtains hung at the windows and a gingham tablecloth covered the small table in the corner.

Dark blue throw pillows were thrown on the bed for accent and a cobalt-blue vase filled with fresh flowers had been moved from the table to the top of the dresser. The paintings on the wall mixed the shades of blue to tie everything all together in a lovely, peaceful atmosphere.

But there was certainly no peace in Alyssa as she now entered the room. She immediately spied the briefcase on the table. She knew it probably contained reports on the murders that had taken place in Cherokee Corners. She didn't want to touch it, didn't want to even get close to it. She was afraid of what might happen.

She turned on the bedside lamp and searched in her pocket for the mints she would set on the pillow after she turned down the blankets and prepared the bed for night.

She placed the mints on the nightstand, then folded down the bedspread, exposing crisp pale blue sheets. A headache began across the front of her forehead, a frighteningly familiar headache.

Knowing she needed to get out of the room as

quickly as possible, she grabbed the mints and placed them on the pillow.

The instant her fingers made contact with the pale blue pillowcase, she froze, blinded by the vision that swooped over her more swiftly, more vividly than any she'd ever suffered before.

She was in the bed…amid the pale blue sheets, but she wasn't alone. Nick was with her, his naked body pressed against hers. She could feel the warmth of the solid muscle of his chest against hers and taste the fire in his lips as his mouth took possession of her own.

His hands were everywhere, stroking across her breasts, moving down her ribs, sliding across her hips and creating fiery flames wherever he touched.

It was like nothing she'd ever experienced before…heights of splendor she'd never climbed. As quickly as a blink of an eye, the scene in her head changed.

She and Nick were no longer in between the pale blue sheets, but rather someplace outside. She recognized nothing about the area, saw a misshapen tree in the distance and smelled the odor of an approaching storm.

In this scene, she and Nick weren't making love, although she straddled him like a lover. Gripped in her hand was the longest, sharpest knife she'd ever seen and she plunged it over and over again into Nick's chest.

Blood splattered as she hit him again and again with a strength she didn't know she possessed. Each time the knife disappeared into his chest a surge of power filled her...a frightening, overwhelming and seductive power.

"Are you all right?"

The deep, male voice pierced through the vision of blood and death and she jumped and whirled around to see Nick standing in the doorway.

It took a moment for her to separate vision from reality. There was a time when her visions left her feeling oddly refreshed and invigorated, but lately they left her drained and half-dizzy, as if she remained in a sort of limbo between the surreal world and the real one.

She knew he had spoken to her, could tell by the look on his face that he awaited a reply. But she couldn't remember what he'd asked her.

She stepped away from his bed, her knees threatening to buckle beneath her. "Excuse me?"

Those eyes of his, those intelligent, intense blue eyes held her gaze for what seemed like an eternity. "I asked if you were all right."

He stepped into the room, closer to her, close enough that she could smell the scent of his cologne. It was a familiar scent. She'd smelled it only moments before when she'd had the vision of the two of them in bed.

"Of course...I was just doing your turndown service."

He eyed her skeptically. "I stood in the doorway and watched you for almost five minutes. You were frozen like a statue. Are you an epileptic? Do you suffer from seizures?''

Her initial instinct was to tell the truth and say no. But then she realized that might be a perfectly good explanation for the visions she knew would be increasing because of his nearness.

"Yes...I suffer from petit mal seizures," she said, hoping she wouldn't be punished for the tiny white lie.

"Are you okay now? Do you need me to get you anything?''

"No, I'm fine.'' What she needed more than anything was to escape this room and his presence.

She still felt the impending doom that the vision had left behind. She feared that Nick Mead's arrival to the town of Cherokee Corners had put into motion events that would forever change her life.

Chapter 3

It was still dark outside when Alyssa pulled herself out of bed the next morning, still dark when she finished showering and got dressed.

Exhaustion weighed her down as she left her small, private quarters and entered the large kitchen. Now she would begin the process of baking muffins and biscuits, browning sausage and frying bacon and all the other tasks that would result in a breakfast to remember at the Redbud Bed-and-Breakfast.

There had been a time when she'd done these chores with joy, but lately the daily grind was beginning to take its toll on her. She was tired, tired all the time, but this morning the weariness weighed heavier than usual.

Of course, it didn't help that she got very little sleep the night before, she thought as she rolled out the dough for biscuits. Knowing Nick Mead was beneath her roof had kept sleep at bay.

As she worked, she thought about the handsome FBI agent. Just because she'd had horrible visions about him didn't mean they would come true. She'd long ago learned not to take what she saw in them at face value.

Sometimes they were just what they were, but other times they were filled with symbolism and meaning she only understood after the events in the vision had come to pass.

But, no matter how she twisted and turned the images her latest vision contained, they still frightened her, especially now that the man in her vision was here in town.

She tried to shove thoughts of Nick and her visions out of her head as she worked. She needed to concentrate on what she was doing in order to make the kind of meal guests had come to expect from her.

Dawn was breaking in the east, a sliver of light peeking over the last of the night clouds when she sat at the island with a cup of coffee.

It was almost six and even though breakfast officially started being served then, guests were rarely up that early. It was usually seven before anyone appeared in the dining room.

This was Alyssa's favorite time of day, when all the preparations for breakfast were finished and she had these few precious moments to sit and reflect.

It was at this time of the morning when whisper-thin memories of her mother visited her. There were few memories, as Alyssa had lost her mother when she'd been four. But she still remembered a familiar scent, a sweet voice and loving hands roughened from basket weaving.

Her grandmother had been a basket weaver, as well. Alyssa had lived with her maternal grandmother until she was eleven, then her grandmother had passed away and Alyssa had been taken into the James family and raised with Savannah, Breanna and Clay by the loving, exuberant Rita Birdsong James and her husband, Thomas.

"Good morning."

She gasped and tensed at the familiar deep voice. She turned on her stool to see Nick standing hesitantly in the kitchen doorway.

If she'd thought he looked handsome the night before, today he practically made her breathless. Clad in a lightweight, light gray suit, he looked coolly professional. "Something smells wonderful," he said.

"If you'll take a seat in the dining room, I'll be glad to bring you some breakfast," she replied.

"Actually, a cup of coffee will do me just fine for the moment." Without waiting for an invitation, he walked over to the coffeemaker, poured himself a cup of coffee, then carried it over and sat on the stool next to hers at the kitchen island.

He was close enough to her that she could smell the scent of a subtle expensive cologne, see the long, individual lashes that framed those startling blue eyes of his.

Before his bottom was firmly planted on the stool,

she jumped up from hers, not wanting to be near him. "Would you care for a muffin or something to eat with your coffee?"

There was a small part of her that resented that he was an early riser, that his presence had cut short the time she always allowed herself to just sit and relax.

There was a small part of her that resented that instead of sitting in the dining room like other guests, he'd invited himself into the kitchen area and poured himself a cup of coffee.

"No, thanks. I'm not much of a morning eater," he replied, looking as comfortable as if he'd spent the last five years' worth of mornings sitting in her kitchen.

"If you aren't a breakfast eater, then you probably would have been better off getting a room at the motel out by the highway. It would have been cheaper." She sounded like a disgruntled crab even to her own ears.

"Yeah, but they don't offer turndown service." His eyes twinkled, and there was a tone to his voice as if he was trying to flirt with her.

She turned her back and stirred a pot of gravy warming on the stove. Drat the man anyway. The last thing she wanted was him flirting with her. The last thing she needed was him having anything to do with her.

"I really prefer if my guests stay out of the kitchen," she said as she turned back to face him. "You understand, liability reasons."

"Of course," he said, but didn't make a move to

stand. He took a sip of his coffee, his gaze lingering on her. "You intrigue me, Ms. Whitefeather. I sometimes stay at bed-and-breakfast establishments, and most of the time I find the proprietors cheerful and friendly, or motherly, or overeager to please. You don't seem to fit the mold."

His words made Alyssa realize just how odd and unfriendly she'd been around him. Perhaps she was drawing more attention to herself from him than necessary by being so distant and cool.

"I apologize," she said and forced herself to sit on the stool next to him once again. "I'm usually not unfriendly, although I can tell you I have never wanted to mother any of my guests. You've just caught me at a bad time…with the murders happening in town and all."

Instantly, whatever twinkle had lightened his eyes was doused. Instead, his eyes turned cold, like chunks of blue ice. "It's been my experience that a murderer on the loose makes everyone on edge."

He stood, grabbed his coffee cup and smiled. "And now I'll go into the dining room like a proper guest should do."

She breathed a sigh of relief as he left the kitchen. Her stomach had been in a knot since the moment he had said good morning. It was the visions, she told herself, and the fear of what might happen, that created the twist in her tummy. It had nothing to do with the fact that he was as handsome as the devil and charming as could be.

Within a half an hour the Harolds had joined Nick.

The Harolds were a couple from Kansas City who were staying in the green room. They had been here for two nights and were checking out at noon that day.

As Alyssa filled the table with an array of breakfast foods, she listened to how easily Nick conversed with the older couple on a variety of topics.

He was as charming with them as he'd been with her and that made her feel better. He probably hadn't been flirting with her at all, he'd just been being himself and that just happened to be exceptionally charismatic.

Within thirty minutes Virginia Maxwell had joined the group. Virginia, a pretty blonde, was the wife of the first victim of the serial killer. She'd moved into the bed-and-breakfast almost immediately after her husband's murder, and was staying in the pink room.

The fourth person who rented a room from Alyssa rarely made it down for breakfast with anyone else. Michael Stanmeyer was something of a recluse. He'd been a guest of Alyssa's for the past two years and he usually came down the stairs to the dining room after all the other guests had eaten.

From the kitchen, she heard Nick's deep voice, although she couldn't make out what he had said, but Virginia's peals of tinkling laughter grated on her nerves.

In the three months Virginia had stayed here, Alyssa had found herself alternating between feeling sorry for the pretty woman and wanting to wring her neck.

She gathered up the last of the freshly baked biscuits and took them out to set on the table. "So, Ms. Whitefeather, when do you eat breakfast?" Nick asked.

"Ms. Whitefeather...my, how formal. Call her Alyssa and you can call me Virginia," Virginia said. "And this is Dave and Cindy." She gestured to the couple, who beamed at Nick with smiles that looked surprisingly alike. "And even though you'll probably never see him, weird Michael is in the purple room."

"Weird Michael?" Nick raised a dark eyebrow quizzically and looked at Alyssa.

"Michael Stanmeyer, and he isn't weird. He's just extremely shy." Alyssa wanted to glare at Virginia, but instead she kept her focus on Nick. "Mr. Stanmeyer is a very nice man."

"Speaking of nice men..." Nick looked at his watch and pushed away from the table. "I've got a couple of my friends to meet. I hope you all have a pleasant day."

Alyssa could have sworn his gaze lingered on her for just a moment longer than on the others and she felt the beginning of a headache thrum at her temples.

No, she thought desperately. She was not going to have a vision...not here...not now. She had to control it. She had to suppress it. She'd done it before, felt the pressure of a vision trying to get through and had managed to back it away.

What she needed to do was get away...escape to the isolation of the kitchen where she could focus on refusing the vision entry into her mind.

"Excuse me, I forgot something…" She ran for the kitchen and sat on the stool where she had been sitting when Nick had first entered the room.

Gripping the edge of the countertop, she closed her eyes and fought against the dizzying blackness that sought to possess her. "No," she whispered, the words a half sob.

But, no matter how hard she fought, the blackness came and immediately following the dark was a vision…the vision. Nick's lips on hers, his hands stroking heat into every area he touched and finally her begging him to take her, to make love to her.

Then, as always happened, the scene changed, transformed into something ugly and violent. Nick's face twisted with surprise and pain as she stabbed him and his blood splattered.

She came to on the kitchen floor, her hip aching from where she must have banged it when she slipped from the stool.

She had no idea how long she'd been unconscious, but she could still hear the sounds of the guests chatting and laughing in the dining room. Thank goodness. Nobody had seen. Nobody knew.

Two in two days. That wasn't a good sign. She'd never had two visions so close together, first the one last night as she'd touched the bed where Nick would be sleeping, and now this one. Two in two days.

She had a feeling Nick's presence had stirred the psychic winds and they were blowing cold through her one right after another.

* * *

The Cherokee Corners Police Station was housed in a low brick building that looked relatively new, but Nick supposed that was the glory of brick...it always managed to look relatively new. It was located two blocks off the city square on a quiet tree-lined street.

His two-man team was already waiting for him, sitting in the confines of the air-conditioning in Bud's sports car. They both got out of the car as Nick pulled into the parking space beside them.

<u>Bud Johnson</u>, a tall, good-looking man with streaked blond hair, grinned at Nick. "There he is, looking fine and fit. Probably just ate a big breakfast at that fancy bed-and-breakfast he's staying at."

Nick nodded. "Eggs and toast, biscuits and gravy, muffins the size of your fist and all the sausage and bacon I could eat."

"You pig," <u>Tony Marcelli</u> exclaimed. Tony was a handsome man with two ex-wives that he claimed were bleeding him dry with alimony payments. "We had a couple of stale doughnuts and a cup of the worst coffee I've ever tasted."

"I highly recommend Ruby's Café for your dining needs. I ate there yesterday for lunch and dinner, and both meals were terrific," Nick replied.

As if on cue the three of them turned and faced the police station. "Well, guess it's time to go meet the locals," Nick said.

Together the three of them entered the police station. The man behind the front desk eyed them curiously. "We're here to see <u>Chief Glen Cleburg,</u>" Nick said and flashed his badge.

"Oh sure." The officer rose and opened the secured door that led down a hallway. "The chief's office is the second door on the left. He's waiting for you."

Nick led his team down the hallway to the closed door. He knocked and waited for a response, then opened and met the man he'd be working with for however long it took to catch their killer.

Glen Cleburg was a big man with graying dark hair and hazel eyes. Lines of stress bracketed his thin lips.

Initial introductions were made, then the men got right down to business. "We'd like to set up a six-man task force, including the three of us and three men from your department," Nick explained. The chief nodded. "Perhaps you have suggestions as to who you want on the team."

"Definitely <u>Clay James,</u>" Cleburg said without hesitation. "He's head of our crime scene unit and is as bright as they come. He even runs a small lab in the back of the building."

"You have a crime scene unit here in Cherokee Corners?" Bud asked in surprise. It was rare for a town so small to have trained crime scene investigators and particularly ones trained in forensic science.

"Yes, my predecessor, Thomas James, foresaw Cherokee Corners growing into a town that would eventually need well-trained police officers in all areas of law enforcement. I encourage my men to get all the education they can."

"That's commendable, sir," Nick replied.

"As far as the other two members of the team, I'll leave that up to Clay's discretion. He can decide who he wants working with you." Glen rose from his desk and motioned for them to follow him out of the office.

"I've set up a room for you to use. Unfortunately, space is not a commodity around here, so the room is rather small, but it's the only place I could free up indefinitely."

They all followed Cleburg down the hall to a room that had apparently been used as a classroom of sorts. It was, indeed, small, but one wall held a blackboard, and the other held a corkboard. It would be perfect for how Nick liked to work his task forces.

"I've had a separate phone and fax line put in and I'm having some of the other officers bring in a couple of computers for your use." Glen frowned. "Unfortunately, you'll find our computer system rudimentary. We've just gone from paper files to computers in the last couple of months and the automation is an ongoing process."

"We'll manage," Nick assured him. Each of the agents had his own personal computer tied into every main computer for sharing information among law officials across the country. "What I'd like to do now is meet Clay James and get started."

"Of course," Glen said quickly. Again he gestured them down the hallway. "I must warn you, Clay is long on smarts, but sometimes he's short on patience and social skills."

"We're used to that sort with Tony here," Bud

said. ''He's our resident Neanderthal man.'' He clapped Tony on the back.

Nick smiled at the interplay between the two men who had been partners for the last five years. The three of them worked well together, often played hard together and despite their teasing, held one another in great esteem. Nick only hoped the three men that would join them from the Cherokee Corners personnel would work well with them also.

They found Clay James seated at a desk in the lab area. He looked up as they entered, a frown of irritation crossing his darkly handsome face. It was there only a moment then gone as he eyed the three men that accompanied his chief. He stood.

''Clay, these men are the FBI agents that are going to work the task force.'' Again introductions were made and hands were shaken.

As Nick gripped Clay in a firm handshake, he saw in the man's dark eyes a keen intelligence that assured him he would be a good addition to their team. He also noticed the black, shiny hair, the equally black eyes and the burnished skin tones that instantly made him think of Alyssa Whitefeather.

He'd hoped to win a smile from her this morning. He wasn't sure why it had become important to him, but he wanted to see her smile. He wanted to see those lush lips of hers curve upward and a spark light the depths of her velvet-blue eyes.

She'd looked so pretty that morning when he'd first seen her from the doorway. Wearing a pale yellow sundress, as she was, and with her hair tied at the nape of her neck with a matching yellow ribbon, he'd wanted to sneak up behind her and place his lips on the vulnerable bared skin just beside her gathered hair.

He yanked his thoughts back to the moment. "Nice to meet you," he said to Clay James. "What we're wanting to put together here is a six-man task force consisting of the three of us and you and two other Cherokee Corners officers."

"I told them you can decide who you want working with you, Clay," Glen said. "Maybe Collins and Sheller or Cavannaugh or Winter."

"Not Sheller," Clay said with a definite tone of voice. "Collins and Winter will be fine."

"I'll leave you two to get to work," Glen said. "But I want to make it clear that I expect to be updated daily and want to be aware of everything concerning these murders." He turned on his heel and disappeared down the hallway.

"The chief showed me the room where we'll be working. Do you want to gather up your other men and meet us in there?" Nick asked. "We'd like to get set up and at work immediately."

Clay nodded. "I'll find the other two officers and we'll meet you in there in about ten minutes."

The men parted, Bud and Tony following behind Nick as they headed back out the front door of the police station. "We'll get our equipment inside and set up, then spend the afternoon going over the files," Nick said.

The other two men nodded and headed for their car while Nick went to his own. From the back seat he grabbed the case that held his computer and his brief-case, then went inside to the room where Glen had said they could set up the team.

In the room, the first thing he did was place a long table in the center. This would be the pulse of the room, where he knew in the coming days the men would spend far too much time going over facts, spec-ulating on possibilities and brainstorming together.

Another long table he placed against the back wall, where computers would be up and running, logged into systems that would tell them about similar crimes and the background of potential suspects, among other things.

He'd just started tacking up photos of the victims, when Clay and his two men entered the room. Clay introduced Nick to Simon Collins and John Winter. Collins was tall, pale, with sandy hair and a ready grin. John Winter looked Native American, his dark features expressing less openness than Collins, but still a reserved friendliness.

When Bud and Tony entered the room, introduc-tions were made all the way around, then everyone got to work. By noon they had the room set up as a sort of war room. The corkboard held the victim and crime scene photos. Computers were plugged in and at the ready and a phone number had been established for the phone line, another for the fax line.

Nick looked around in satisfaction. They were ready to begin the process of finding a killer. The men were all seated at the table in the center of the room looking at Nick expectantly. ''It's vitally important that the six of us work as a team. I don't believe in egos getting in the way of the investigation. We work this as a team and we solve it as a team.''

He sensed the others' satisfaction with his words. He'd worked too many task forces, and in his experience had learned that there was no room for hotshots. He had no patience for men who worked for personal gain instead of for the common good of the team to achieve their objective.

''We all sit at this table with strengths and weaknesses,'' Nick continued. ''Clay, you and John and Simon bring to the table the fact that this is your town. You know it and the people and that's vital if the killer is a local.''

For the next several hours the men reviewed the facts of each murder, discussing the victims, the circumstances surrounding the deaths and any forensic evidence that had been found.

It was after five when they wound up. ''We'll make it an early day today,'' Nick said. ''But, I'll warn you in advance, you might want to tell your wife, your girlfriend or your significant other that from here on out you're on duty twenty-four hours a day. We'll be working long hours and I'll want each one of us to carry cell phones so we're only a call away from one another at any time of the day or night.''

As the men gathered up their paperwork and got ready to leave, Nick turned to Clay. ''Can I buy you a drink?'' Nick figured it wouldn't hurt to foster a little goodwill with the man who he knew would probably prove invaluable to the team.

"Sure," Clay replied. "A beer would taste good right now."

The two men walked out of the police station together. "You'll have to help me out here. Since I've been in town, the only place I've been is to Ruby's Café and I didn't notice beer on the menu."

Clay smiled. "No, but if you go in after six at night, you'll probably smell it on her breath. The best place for a beer and a little quiet talk is Sanford's. It's just down the block. We can walk there."

For a moment the two men walked in silence. Nick had already sized Clay up as a highly intelligent man with a knack for finding evidence when none seemed to have been left behind. He had a feeling Clay still hadn't made up his mind about what kind of man Nick might be.

That was all right. Nick didn't trust a man who jumped to conclusions too quickly. "Heard your family recently went through a pretty traumatic experience," Nick said.

Clay looked at him in surprise. "Where'd you hear that?"

"When I spoke with Chief Cleburg initially he told me that he intended for you to work with me and he told me about your mother's kidnapping. He also told me that if it hadn't been for your stubborn diligence and work, she might have never been found."

"Thankfully, we found her before she suffered any physical harm," Clay replied.

"How's she doing now?"

Clay's mouth curved up in a grin. "You'd have to

know my mother to understand that she's a survivor. She's exactly like she was before the kidnapping…enjoying life and her family.''

''That's good to hear,'' Nick said as they entered the darkened interior of Sanford's. It was a typical small-town tavern, with pool tables in the back, a layer of thick smoke hanging in the air and a bar counter that had probably felt a thousand elbows resting on it.

Clay motioned to the bar and the two men slid onto stools. They ordered their drinks from a burly bartender who appeared to double as bouncer, as well.

''Are you staying out at the motel?'' Clay asked.

''No, I'm staying at the Redbud Bed-and-Breakfast here on the square,'' Nick replied.

''Ah, my cousin's place.''

Nick looked at him in surprise. ''Alyssa Whitefeather is your cousin?''

''A close cousin. My mother raised her from the time she was eleven. She's more like another sister than a cousin.'' Clay took a sip of his beer, then continued. ''I want you to know I intend to put all my time and energy into finding the bastard who's killing the men of our town,'' Clay said. ''But the first thing I need to do is request Saturday off duty. I'm getting married that day.''

''Married? And you're just asking for one day off?''

''My fiancée, Tamara, knows how important this case is. I've promised her a real honeymoon when we catch this creep.'' Clay wrapped his hands around his beer glass. "You know, most of the town is going to turn out for the wedding. Maybe you should come, see the town people at play."

"I wouldn't want to intrude on such a personal ceremony," Nick protested.

"Trust me, it wouldn't be an intrusion, but if you are uncomfortable coming alone, I'll set it up with Alyssa and the two of you can come together."

Nick instantly felt a spike in his adrenaline, although he fought to keep his enthusiasm for the idea out of his voice. "Isn't it possible she might already have an escort?"

"Alyssa? Nah, she never dates. I'm sure she's planning on going alone."

"Then that would be great. I could have a look at the folks there and won't feel so out of place if I'm with a family member."

"Then consider it done. I'll call Alyssa tonight and set it up with her."

"Alyssa...is she on medication for her epilepsy?" Nick asked.

There was no mistaking the blank look in Clay's dark eyes. "Epilepsy?" he repeated slowly, as if the word was utterly foreign to his vocabulary.

"Yeah, I walked in on her last night and she was, like, in a trance. I asked her if she had epilepsy and was having some sort of seizure and she said yes."

"So, she told you she has epilepsy? No, she isn't on any kind of medication." Clay lifted the beer glass to his lips, his gaze focused away from Nick.

And in that instant Nick suspected that Alyssa

Whitefeather didn't have epilepsy at all. She'd lied to him, and Clay was merely trying to cover her tracks. Interesting.

If she didn't have epilepsy...if she hadn't been suffering a petit mal seizure when he'd seen her in his room the night before, then what had she been doing? Why had she appeared like a woman in a trance...a woman completely gone from the real world and its surroundings?

The only answer could be she was hiding something from him. But why?

Chapter 4

Livid and a little bit afraid…it was the only way to describe the emotions that roared through Alyssa as she dressed for Clay and Tamara's wedding early Saturday morning.

She couldn't believe that Clay had manipulated her into bringing Nick along. She didn't want to go with him, didn't want to spend any time in his company. She wanted nothing at all to do with the man.

It was bad enough that for the last two mornings he'd been the first one up, forcing her to interact with him without buffers between them. She'd been pleasant but short, not encouraging small talk.

However, that didn't keep her from being intensely aware of his every movement when she served him in the mornings. Despite his initial claim not to be a breakfast eater, for the last two mornings he'd enjoyed a big serving of her biscuits and gravy. He was a neat eater, never leaving behind a mess.

Neat eater or not, as far as she was concerned, it was vital that she keep as much distance from the man as possible. Her plan for the day was to escort him to the wedding, introduce him to people, then leave him to his own devices until the wedding celebration was over.

As she brushed her hair, she realized that it was difficult to hang on to her foul mood. It was rare she took a day off and even more rare that she got to enjoy a traditional ceremony with friends and loved ones.

Mary had agreed to come in this morning and take care of the breakfast preparations and run the business for the entire day, leaving Alyssa free to simply enjoy the wedding of her best friend, Tamara Greystone, and her cousin, Clay.

She finished brushing her hair and stepped back from the mirror, eyeing her reflection critically. She had considered wearing a traditional Cherokee tear dress, but at the last minute had changed her mind.

There would be plenty of people wearing traditional clothing today, but Alyssa had opted for a cool mint-green sundress. Dainty white hoops decorated her earlobes and white sandals completed the outfit.

She looked at her watch. Almost eight. It was time to go. Nick had been surprised when she'd told him the night before that she would be leaving the house around eight in the morning.

She had a feeling he had no idea what he was in

for, had probably never experienced a traditional Cherokee wedding ceremony. As far as Alyssa was concerned, there was nothing more beautiful, more spiritual and filled with more community bonding than a Cherokee wedding.

Looking at her watch again, she realized she couldn't put it off any longer. It was time to leave her private quarters and take Nick to a wedding.

He was waiting for her in the front foyer, looking cool and far too sexy in a beige, lightweight suit that complemented his blue eyes and dark hair. "Ready?" she asked briskly.

His gaze swept her, beginning at the top of her hair, down to the sandals on her feet, and a smile of appreciation turned his lips upward into one of his sexy smiles. "I'll be the most envied man at the wedding," he said.

Despite her desire to the contrary, Alyssa felt the warmth of a blush sweep over her features. "Thank you," she murmured.

"I'll drive if you'll provide directions to the church."

He pulled his car keys out of his pocket.

"All right, but we aren't going to a church."

Together they left by the back door, where his car was parked in the small lot behind the bed-and-breakfast. "Where are we going if not to a church?" he asked.

"The Cherokee Cultural Center," she replied. "Clay and Tamara are being married in a traditional ceremony." She tried not to freeze as he opened the passenger door for her, standing close enough that she could smell his cologne but not so close that they might inadvertently touch.

She didn't want him to touch her in any way, was afraid a single touch might bring on the vision and she wanted nothing to mar the happiness of the day.

She slid into her seat and watched as he walked around the front of the car to the driver's side. His suit hung on him as if it had been made to fit his broad shoulders and slender hips.

She grabbed her seat belt and buckled it around her. A man as handsome as he was would be married. He probably had a good woman and two or three kids at home, waiting for him to return from his field trip. Meanwhile, he probably flirted with every female in sight when he was in the field, or had meaningless affairs while away from home.

By the time he slid in behind the steering wheel, Alyssa was working up a case against him, anything to keep him at a mental and physical distance.

"All set?" he asked as he fastened his seat belt.

She nodded. "Get on Main Street and head north," she said.

"You mentioned that Clay and his fiancée are being married in a traditional ceremony. What does that mean?" he asked once they were on Main Street.

"It's not only a beautiful ceremony, but lots of preparation has gone into it before the actual ceremony begins," she replied. "The place for the ceremony is blessed for seven consecutive days. A sacred fire burns, and before the ceremony begins all the guests are blessed, as well.''

"Sounds fascinating," he said.

What she found fascinating was the scent of him that filled the car interior. It was a distinctly male scent of his cologne mingling with a hint of shaving cream.

"I have to warn you," she said. "It will be a long day. Following the actual ceremony itself will be singing and dancing and feasting into the night. If you decide you want to leave early, please don't worry about me. There will be lots of people there who can bring me home when I'm ready to come home.''

He cast her a sideways glance, his expression teasing. "We haven't even gotten there yet and already you're trying to ditch me. What kind of a date is that?"

Again she felt the warmth of a blush sweep up her neck, and to her consternation her pulse rate raced a little faster. "This isn't a date. It's a favor for Clay and my contribution in helping find the killer that's loose in the town.''

"Clay mentioned that you don't date."

"I don't have time." Her words were clipped and brusque. It irritated her that he and Clay had talked about her dating habits, or lack thereof.

"If you don't date, then how do you intend to find Mr. Right?''

Although his question was innocent enough, it stirred a wistfulness inside her. She was twenty-nine years old and at this moment in her life she didn't have time to find a Mr. Wrong, let alone a man she wanted to spend the rest of her life with. Besides, she'd known from a very early age that there would probably be no Mr. Right for her, that it was her destiny to be alone, to live alone.

"What makes you think I'm interested in finding a Mr. Right?" she finally asked in answer to his question.

He shrugged his broad shoulders. "I thought that's what all women want."

"That's the most chauvinistic thing I've ever heard," she replied.

He laughed, a pleasant low rumble that stirred something inside her and once again made her heart race just a little faster. "Not really, because I think the same thing is true about men. All they really want is the love of a good woman in their lives."

She eyed him curiously. "And do you have that? Are you married, Nick?"

"No." The single word shot out of him and she thought his hands tightened perceptibly on the steering wheel.

Divorced, she thought, and by his reaction to the question it had probably been a nasty divorce. She was grateful when the cultural center came into view.

"Clay wasn't kidding when he said practically everyone in town would be here today," he said as he angled his car into one of the last parking spaces in the lot.

"The people of Cherokee Corners love a good party," she said. She didn't wait for him to open her car door. The moment the car came to a full stop, she unbuckled her seat belt and got out.

When he exited the car and they began to walk toward the building, she remained far enough away from him that he couldn't take her arm or touch her in any way.

"Should I have put on more deodorant this morning?" he asked, obviously noticing her distance.

"No, you're fine." She steeled herself and moved closer to him. It was highly probable that at some point throughout the day they would touch. Shoulders might bump, hands might brush…she simply had to prepare herself for such an event.

The sound of laughter and chatter filled the air. It was a day of celebration, she reminded herself. Tamara and Clay would join their lives together today. Most of the townspeople would be here for the joyous event. It was not a day for visions of death. She refused to allow any visions to ruin the day.

To test herself and her inner strength, on impulse she reached out and grabbed Nick's hand. "Come on, I'll give you a quick tour of the building before we join the party in the back."

"All right," he agreed. His strong fingers closed around her hand and she breathed a grateful sigh.

She felt no approaching darkness, no headache edging its way through her brain. She felt nothing except a seductive warmth flooding through her from their point of contact.

When they entered the building, she broke the physical contact between them. She wasn't sure why, but she found touching Nick almost as disturbing as suffering from one of her visions.

Nick had begun to think that Alyssa Whitefeather had no sense of humor and had never allowed the luxury of a smile to cross her lush lips.

He'd been wrong. After the interesting, educational, but brief, tour of the place, they had stepped out the back doors of the building, where immediately members of her family had greeted her.

It was like a switch had been turned on inside her. He was introduced to Thomas and Rita James, Savannah and Riley Frazier, Breanna and Adam Spencer and a delightful little six-year-old charmer by the name of Maggie.

But, as the introductions were being made and small talk exchanged, Nick was riveted by Alyssa's smile, her laughter and the sparkle that lit up her dark blue eyes.

He'd thought her pretty before, but now he found her positively breathtaking. She drew him to her in a way no woman had since the day he'd met his Dorrie.

Alyssa was beauty and mystery, and now with a smile on her face and her laughter riding the air, she was sunshine, warming him from the inside out.

It was funny, but from the moment he'd first laid eyes on her, he'd felt some sort of weird connection, knew that one way or another she was going to play a role in his time here in Cherokee Corners.

By ten o'clock the crowd had swelled to massive proportions and Nick reluctantly left Alyssa's side to mingle and keep an eye out for anyone who might fit the profile of the killer that he was putting together.

He introduced himself as a friend of Alyssa's, insinuated himself into conversations and mentally made notes of the faces and names who could possibly be the killer or the next potential victim.

If the killer wasn't a local their task would be even more difficult because during the summer months there were plenty of tourists in town, plenty of strange faces visiting from different places.

He made his way back to Alyssa's side as the ceremony began. Despite the heat of the day, a huge fire burned in the center of the area. An elderly Cherokee appeared and a reverent silence fell over the audience.

"That's the priest from the reservation," Alyssa explained to Nick. In the center of the circle that the guests formed stood Clay James and his bride-to-be.

Clay looked proud and handsome, wearing a pair of dress slacks and a shirt with turquoise and coral ribbonlike material woven into the cotton. Tamara was in what Alyssa told him was a traditional tear dress. It was white with turquoise- and coral-colored triangles around the yoke and hem.

Rita stood beside them. Because Cherokee society was matrilineal and the woman held the family clan, Rita represented Tamara as a clan mother.

The priest went around the circle of people, blessing them, then returned to Clay and Tamara and blessed them, as well. The priest covered Clay in a blue blanket and Tamara in another blue one.

Chants were chanted and songs were sung and Nick enjoyed the beauty of the language of the Cherokee.

"The separate blankets portray their separate lives before their union," Alyssa said softly from beside him.

As he continued to watch, the priest removed the blankets from the two and covered them both with a white blanket. Once again he chanted in the beautiful Cherokee language.

"This signifies the beginning of their new life together," Alyssa said.

He noticed the shine of tears of happiness in her eyes as she spoke. A flutter of warmth swept through him. He'd always been a sucker for women who cried at weddings.

When the priest removed the white blanket from the married couple, the crowd cheered. Tamara looked up at her new husband and even from the distance where he stood, Nick saw the light in her eyes...the light that said that Clay was her one and only love.

Nick remembered that look. He remembered the look and the feelings that went along with it...the wonder of love found, the joy of love reciprocated, the glory of love committed forever and ever.

He remembered the feeling of loving somebody more than anything and anyone on the face of the earth, of wanting to take care of her, make her smile and be a part of her world forever. It was a heady feeling, and that was part of what had been missing in his life since Dorrie's death.

Murphy had not only stolen Dorrie's life, he'd taken much, much more from Nick, and sooner or later Nick would find the man and make him pay.

Again he reminded himself that he wasn't in Cherokee Corners hunting for Murphy, but rather another serial killer, one who was killing vital young men and leaving them naked in plain sight.

Following the actual ceremony began the dancing and feasting. As Nick mingled with the crowd, he didn't forget his reason for being here, although it would have been easy to get caught up in the festivities and Alyssa's lovely animation.

He ate food he'd never tasted before, visited with people he'd never met before and thought of the victims who were not here to celebrate with the rest of their town.

Greg Maxwell. Sam McClane. Tim O'Brien. And the latest victim, Jonathon Blackbird. Four men in the prime of their lives, killed, and their voices cried out to Nick, cried out for resolution and closure.

Throughout the festivities, no matter how engrossed in conversation, no matter how deep in thought he became, his gaze continued to seek out Alyssa.

He watched as she performed a traditional dance with some of the other Cherokee men and women. She'd kicked off her sandals and the drums beat with a contagious rhythm.

As she danced, her hair flew wild around her, laughter bubbled from her lips and he wanted to be there next to her, dancing in the way of her people, sharing the laughter with her.

He also couldn't help but notice that the sundress she wore fit her like a glove, accentuating the thrust of her breasts and emphasizing a slender waist. A flicker of desire had begun in the pit of his stomach from almost the first moment he'd seen her and today that fire had begun to burn more intensely.

It was strange, because he hadn't felt desire for anyone for a very long time. It was odd that a woman who had been less than friendly to him in the brief time he'd known her was the one who had brought that part of him alive once again.

The other fact he found intriguing was that she rarely left her family's side. If she wasn't near one of her "sisters," she was near the other or standing close to Rita.

It was nearing dusk when she approached where he stood talking to a couple of Cherokee Corners police officers. It had taken him only moments upon meeting Officer Jason Sheller to realize why Clay hadn't wanted him on the task force.

The young man talked too much, tried too hard and had an air of desperation about him. The other officer, Fred Tarleton seemed to be a nice enough man, but didn't seem to have the sharp, keen intelligence of the men Clay had chosen for the task force.

He watched as Alyssa drew near. Her feet were dusty, her hair in disarray, but she carried the sparkle of a wonderful day on her face. He excused himself from the two officers and turned to face Alyssa.

"I don't know about you, but I'm ready to go," she said, then frowned. "But, if you'd like to stay longer, I can catch a ride from somebody else."

He smiled. "First you tell me if I want to leave early, you'll catch another ride. Now you're saying if I want to stay later, you'll catch another ride. Are you intentionally trying to confuse me?"

For the first time, that full-wattage smile of hers was directed at him and he felt it like a punch in his midsection. "Are you that easily confused?"

Yes, he wanted to say. Her smile for him and the gentle teasing in her voice confused the hell out of him. "Not usually," he replied, then added, "and I'm ready to go, too."

Together they left the cultural center and walked toward where his car was parked. As they walked, a group of children ran by them.

"A-tsa-s-gi-li!" One of the young boys yelled. The others giggled and they all ran faster.

"What was that all about?" he asked.

"Nothing…just kid stuff," she said.

"What did it mean?" He opened the passenger door for her.

"Witch," she replied. "A-tsa-s-gi-li is the Cherokee word for witch." She scooted into the car.

He closed her door, walked around and slid in behind the steering wheel. "Why would anyone call you a witch?" he asked curiously.

"They were just kids being silly," she replied. "So, what did you think of your first Cherokee wedding?" she asked, changing the subject.

"You were right, it's a beautiful ceremony."

"It was a wonderful day," she agreed. "It was so nice to see all of the family together and happy."

She was more relaxed and more open than she'd been since he'd checked into her establishment. "Your family seems very nice."

"They're my family through default. They took me in when I was eleven."

"Yeah, Clay told me you'd lost your parents when you were young and your aunt Rita and uncle Thomas claimed you as one of their own."

A soft smile played at the corners of her mouth. "I claimed them, as well."

"I didn't realize Clay and his sisters were half-Cherokee," Nick said, hoping he wasn't being politically incorrect.

Alyssa laughed. "Uncle Thomas never lets them forget that they have his proud Irish blood in their veins, but they all look so much like Aunt Rita, it's hard not to think of them as one-hundred percent Cherokee."

"What about you?" he asked.

"One-hundred percent pure American Indian," she replied.

"I was just wondering because of your blue eyes. I would think that unusual."

She smiled. "Apparently our bloodline isn't quite as pure as some of my ancestors claimed. What about you?"

"I'm a mutt," he replied. He realized he was driving slower than usual, enjoying the fact that they were having an actual conversation, even though others might think it an inane one.

"I've heard that mutts make the best kinds of dogs. I'm not sure about what kind of men they make."

He cast her a sideways glance, surprised to see the laughter shining in her eyes. She was teasing him and he loved it. "If you follow the dog theory, it would make me intelligent, easy to train and eager to please."

"And if that was the case, you'd already have a home," she replied.

Unfortunately at that moment they arrived back at the bed-and-breakfast. If he'd had his choice, he'd continue to drive and enjoy her mood for a hundred miles…a thousand miles.

He wanted to keep joking with her and watch the twinkle in her eyes as she responded. He wanted to savor these moments with her, when she was so relaxed and inviting, because he had a feeling once the night ended and tomorrow came, she'd be back to being cool and distant to him.

He pulled into a spot in the back parking lot and shut off the engine. "I'm sorry to see the day end."

She smiled. "Me, too. It was fun." She turned her gaze to the back of the building before them. "But, now it's back to real life."

"Yeah, I guess you're right." He pulled his keys out of the ignition and got out of the car. She got out, as well. As they walked toward the building, Nick grabbed her by the elbow to halt their progress.

"Alyssa, I know you got roped into taking me to

the wedding today by your cousin, but I just wanted
you to know how much I appreciate it.''

She stared at him…no, not at him…through him.
She was perfectly still, frozen in time like a statue of
bronze.

"Alyssa?" He spoke her name softly, not sure
what to do. She must be having one of the petit mal
seizures no one seemed to know about, he thought.

What should he do? Should he call her name
louder? Shake her? Try to pull her out of it? Or was
that dangerous? Was he better off just waiting for it
to pass?

Before he'd made a decision, she uttered a soft
moan, then her eyelids fluttered and closed and her
knees buckled from beneath her.

He managed to grab her before she hit the ground.
He scooped her up in his arms and fumbled in his
pocket for the key that would unlock the back door.

He got her inside and hesitated in the small back
foyer, unsure whether to take her into her private
rooms or up to his. The decision was made quickly.
He didn't have a key to get into her private space so
he carried her up the flight of stairs to the blue bedroom.

Gently, he placed her on the bed. She seemed to
be unconscious. Should he call a doctor? He looked
at the phone on his nightstand, then back at her, unsure what to do. He recognized even in the brief time
he'd known her that she was a fairly private person.
Should he call somebody or not?

He had just reached for the phone, deciding he

couldn't sit and watch her so still a minute longer, when she drew a deep breath and her eyes fluttered open.

She sat up as if jolted by a shock of electricity, then stared at him for a long moment and burst into tears.

"Hey…hey." Nick sat on the bed next to her and took her hands in his. "Alyssa, what's the matter?"

"I'm sorry…I'm so sorry." She hid her face in her hands, sobs racking her body.

"It's all right. There's nothing to apologize for," he exclaimed. He wanted to take her in his arms and make her tears stop.

She had nothing to be ashamed of, nothing to be sorry or embarrassed about. "Alyssa, please don't cry…it's no big deal. You had a little brain glitch, that's all. It's nothing to be sorry for."

She uncovered her face, her gorgeous dark eyes awash with tears. "I'm not crying for me, Nick. I'm crying for you…for your loss."

He frowned, immediately confused. "What are you talking about? What loss?"

She swiped at her tears and shook her head as if weary. "I'm talking about your wife…Dorrie."

Nick froze and stared at her in stunned silence. For a moment all he could hear was the blood as it rushed from his head, the sound filling his ears to the exclusion of everything else.

He watched as she got up off the bed, tears still staining her cheeks as she apparently waited for whatever his response might be.

Nick fought through the sudden flood of memories Dorrie's name had evoked, and with the memories came the rage, a rage that at the moment was directed at the woman who had uttered her name.

He got off the bed and in two strides stood in front of Alyssa. "How do you know about Dorrie?"

Her eyes flickered with a hint of fear, but Nick didn't care. She should be afraid. He didn't know what her game was, but he intended to get to the bottom of it. "Tell me…tell me, dammit." He grabbed her by the shoulders. "What in the hell do you know about Dorrie?"

Chapter 5

She hadn't wanted to tell him. Alyssa saw the confusion in his eyes, felt the bite of anger through the fingertips that pressed into her shoulders.

She shouldn't have said anything, but the new vision had exploded without warning and she'd come out of the darkness filled with pain for Nick and unable to stifle herself before it spewed out of her.

The pleasure of the day had left her too open, too relaxed, vulnerable to the demons of her visions. Her defenses had been down and she'd paid the price.

His eyes demanded answers and reluctantly she tried to give them to him. "I saw her...your wife, lying on a bed in a room, and I saw you weeping, crying her name over and over again." She tried to step back from him, flinching as his fingers bit deeper. "Nick...please...you're hurting me."

He immediately loosened his hold but didn't release her completely. "What do you mean you saw her, saw me? What in the hell are you talking about?"

His eyes still blazed with anger and his breath was hot on her face. This was not the man she'd seen in her vision. That man had been broken, filled with grief too enormous to bear.

She broke eye contact with him and stared down at the floor. "I don't have epilepsy, Nick. I don't have any kind of petit mal seizures. I...I see things."

Although she wasn't looking at him she could feel his stare on her for a long moment, then his hands dropped from her shoulders. Only when he took a step back from her did she look at him once again.

"What do you mean? I don't understand."

"I have visions." She drew a deep breath and fought the impulse to worry the ends of her hair, a nervous habit she'd been trying to break.

"Visions?" He eyed her as if she were speaking a foreign language.

She released her breath with an audible sigh. She hadn't wanted to tell him this. It was a part of herself she tried to keep hidden from others, knowing the reactions were usually negative. He'd think her a nut or some sort of mental case like half the people in this town thought. She knew what to expect and faced him with weary resignation.

"I'm not sure how to explain it to you. I don't understand it myself. I've had visions since I was a child."

He sank down to the bed, the anger in his eyes

dissipating as bewilderment wrinkled his forehead. "Visions? Tell me what you saw just now." He patted the bed next to him. "Come here…sit down and tell me every detail that you can remember about your vision."

Tentatively, she sank down next to him, careful to keep several inches between their bodies even though she knew the possibility of having another vision so quickly was remote.

She clenched her hands together and attempted to remove herself emotionally from the scene she had just witnessed in her mind.

"I saw a woman lying on a bed." She closed her eyes, reaching not for the vision itself, but rather for the memories of the vision. "Blond…her hair is the color of corn silk. She…she is naked…and it's obvious she's dead. There's blood…lots of blood… around her neck…up the wall behind where she is." The horror of the scene made her stop, swallow hard against the rising emotion that threatened to choke in her throat.

"Then you're there," she continued, "crying her name over and over again…Dorrie…Dorrie. Then I see a headstone…Doreen Marie Mead…and the dates."

She opened her eyes and swallowed hard against the tears that once again threatened to fall. Despite her desire to the contrary, the emotions from the scene she'd witnessed swept over her…not her emotions, but his.

Disbelief turned to shock, shock turned to horror

and horror changed to a grief so intense it made her stomach ache.

She wrapped her arms around her stomach and continued. "I know, Nick…I saw. I know your wife was murdered almost three years ago and I'm sorry…so sorry."

Nick still had a stunned look in his eyes…blue eyes she'd never known could appear so dark. She watched and waited for some sort of response from him.

What she wanted to do was take him in her arms, hold him close and tell him how sorry she was for the incredible loss he'd suffered.

She wanted to apologize for thinking him some kind of ladies' man, a shallow flirt, when in fact he'd been a man mourning the tragedy of his wife's vicious murder.

"You could have gotten any of this information from reading newspaper accounts or by doing some kind of Internet search," he said with a touch of belligerence in his voice.

"That's true," she replied evenly. "But I didn't. I didn't know anything about your wife until a few minutes ago when the vision swept over me." She frowned as a new memory of the vision intruded. "There was something else…a strange mark on her chest…it…it looked like the letter M."

Nick gasped and jumped off the bed as if he were a bullet shot from a gun. He stared at her, his look one of stunned surprise more than anything else. "How did you know about that? That piece of information was never released to the press."

"I told you. I saw it." She grabbed a strand of her long hair and twirled it around her finger. "A-tsa-s-gi-li. You asked me earlier what it meant when those children yelled the word at me. I told you they were just silly kids, but this is why they call me witch, because of my visions."

She raised her chin in a show of defiance. "Half the people in this town think I'm a witch. The other half think I'm just plain weird. So, which group do you fall in?"

He raked a hand through his dark hair and drew a deep breath. "I don't think I fall into either group." Once again he sat down on the bed next to her. "So, what you're telling me is that you have some form of psychic ability."

She didn't reply but merely shrugged her shoulders. "I don't know what I have, I only know that there are times when I see things…things from the past…things from the future…and things that never come to pass. I never know for sure when a vision will appear, don't know what causes them or how they will affect me. Sometimes I pass out, sometimes I don't."

"Alyssa, I've seen a lot of things, met a lot of people in my line of work. I'm not a complete un-believer."

A tremendous weight lifted from her shoulders. "Really?"

"Really." He reached out and took one of her hands in his. She tensed, afraid the contact might pro-voke another horrible image, but nothing happened.

"I'm not an unbeliever, but I also have a certain amount of normal skepticism."

"I would expect that from anyone," she said, finding it a little more difficult to concentrate with his warm, strong hand holding hers.

"These visions of yours…are they always so clearcut as the one you just told me about…the one about Dorrie?" he asked.

"No. That one was unusually clear. I don't always get whole pictures, or see things that make sense. Sometimes I interpret them after whatever the vision portends has already happened."

His hand tightened around hers, his gaze holding hers steadily. "It must be frightening for you."

Again she felt as if a weight had been removed, as if he truly understood what so many people did not. "It is," she replied softly. "My grandmother had visions, as well. I lived with her until I was eleven and she told me that people would be afraid of me, or make fun of me or be leery of me. She tried to make me strong. I think she knew what kind of burden this would be."

"Surely your aunt and uncle understood," he replied.

"Aunt Rita and Uncle Thomas were wonderful, as were Savannah, Breanna and Clay. They didn't understand the things I saw, but they accepted it just as if I had epilepsy." She offered him a small smile. "I'm sorry for the lie. I've grown accustomed to trying to protect myself."

He returned her smile and she felt an enticing

warmth stealing through her. "Clay is protective of you, too. When I asked him if you were on medication for your epilepsy, he managed to avoid answering me and not give away your secret."

She laughed. "I can't begin to tell you how many mean, hateful boys Clay beat up for me when we were young."

"So, everyone in town knows about your visions?"

She couldn't help the rueful smile that crossed her lips. "Nick, this is a middle-size town with a small-town rumor mill. Not everyone knows I have visions, but most people know there's something odd about me. They've either heard whispers or rumors about me that keep them at arm's length from me. Of course, there are exceptions…like Mary, who works for me, and Tamara, Clay's new wife, who has become one of my very best friends."

She pulled her hand from his, finding the contact far too pleasurable. "I need to go," she said. She was exhausted, not only from the day's activities, but also from the stress of the vision and their conversation.

She stood and he did, as well. "I'll take care of my own turndown service tonight."

"Thanks." She paused in the doorway. "And thanks, Nick, for not looking at me as if I'm a freak."

He reached out and took the strand of hair she'd begun to twist around her fingers. His nearness made her heart skip a beat. Close…too close…and it wasn't a vision that made her nervous but rather the fact that there was heat radiating from his eyes as he gazed at her.

"You aren't a freak. You're a beautiful woman." Before she could guess his intention, he leaned forward and placed his lips on hers.

The action was so unexpected that she didn't move, didn't pull away. Her reaction was just as unexpected as an instantaneous fireball exploded in the pit of her stomach.

His arms wrapped around her as he deepened the kiss, his tongue tentatively touching the tip of hers, then delving deeper.

For a moment, for just the briefest millisecond in time, Alyssa gave herself to the kiss, to the mastery of his lips plying hers.

And it was mastery…his lips were soft, but slightly demanding, warm but not threateningly so. His scent surrounded her…the utterly masculine scent of the day spent outside. He smelled like hot sun and wood smoke from the day's sacred fire and a hint of the cologne she found so pleasing.

His chest was hard, muscled against her softer breasts, and she wished for more…to feel his naked chest against hers, to feel his mouth tasting every inch of her.

In that instant the vision she'd had of them for the past month exploded in her mind. Making love with Nick…killing Nick…blood everywhere…his blood— She jerked away from him and stumbled out of the room.

She was vaguely aware of him calling her name, but she didn't stop until she'd run down the stairs and locked herself in her own private quarters.

Her lips still burned from the imprint of his mouth against hers, but the pleasure had turned to horror when the reality of what the kiss might have begun hit home.

She hadn't told him about the vision where she made love to him, then killed him.

She sank down on her beige sofa and rubbed her index finger over her mouth. As crazy as it was, she was slightly superstitious. She was afraid to tell him about the disturbing vision, afraid that by speaking about it out loud it might somehow come true.

Definitely she didn't want to kiss Nick, she didn't want to encourage any kind of a relationship with him. She was afraid somehow by doing so she would set into motion the elements that might make the vision come true.

"So, the general profile we're looking at is a male Caucasian probably between the ages of twenty-five and thirty-five. He's organized and intelligent and apparently has some knowledge of forensic science, which is why there hasn't been much physical or transfer evidence found at any of the scenes." Nick turned from the members of the task team to write the pertinent information on the blackboard behind him.

"Not only does he seem to have some knowledge of forensic evidence, I think maybe he's playing games with us, as well," Clay said.

"What do you mean?" Nick turned to face Clay. The newlywed looked tired, but throughout the morn-

ing he'd been as sharp as ever, apparently not allowing any weariness from the day and night before to
affect his thought process.

"I've analyzed the bloody footprint left at the third
murder scene. It appears to be a men's size-twelve
sneaker, but that size foot doesn't correlate with the
weight impact of the print."

"What does that mean for us dumb grunts?" Simon Collins asked.

"If I correlate the weight of the impact print, then
the man we're looking for is at least about five foot
eight to six feet tall and weighs about a hundred and
ten pounds."

"A hundred and ten pounds?" Bud frowned
thoughtfully. "Then this should be easy...we're chas-
ing a skeleton."

"What I think is that it's possible we're dealing
with somebody very crafty," Clay replied.

"You think the scene was staged?" Nick asked
with concern.

"I think it's very possible."

Damn, Nick thought. The footprint had been the
one major piece of evidence they believed the killer
had unintentionally left behind. If it was bogus, left
intentionally to throw them off track, then they had
next to nothing to go on.

"I think we need to go back and revisit each crime,
reinterview family members, reinvestigate everything
we can about the victims. I'll assign you each a victim. I want to know everything about them...the
status of their marriages, their finances, relationships

with co-workers. I want to know what they usually ate for breakfast, where they shopped, where they got their haircuts…everything.''

He paused, waiting for a groan from the three men who had been working the cases before the arrival of his team, but nobody complained. Good. He needed men who would do the work, then do it again, then do it a third time if necessary. ''For the next two days or so you'll get what information you can, then be prepared to give a comprehensive report. There's a pattern here, but so far we haven't put our finger on it. Something ties these four men together. We need to find out what it is.''

He walked over to the corkboard that was decorated with photos of the four victims. ''Bud, why don't you take Greg Maxwell. Simon, you get Sam McClane. John, you take Tim O'Brien, and Tony, you get the latest victim, Jonathon Blackbird. According to the timeline of the murders, and if the killer stays true to that timeline, we're going to have another victim in the next ten days or so.''

He gave the men a few minutes to talk among themselves. ''Clay, I'd like you to be available tomorrow to go over all the forensic evidence you've managed to gather from each scene.''

Clay nodded. ''Unfortunately, that won't take long.''

There was obvious frustration in Clay's voice. Nick knew that kind of frustration. He lived with it every day, every time the name Murphy came into his mind.

''Okay. I think we'll knock off for the day.'' It was

after five and even though Nick knew Clay would work as long as Nick asked him to, Nick hadn't forgotten the man was a newlywed.

Besides, he intended to keep him just a few minutes longer after the others had left. He had some questions to ask him. "Clay, could I talk to you a minute?" he asked as the others were leaving the room. "I promise I won't keep you long."

"Sure," he agreed. He sat with one hip on the table and looked at Nick expectantly.

Nick waited until the others had left the room, then faced Clay. "I know about Alyssa's visions," he said without preamble.

Clay's dark eyes radiated no emotion. "She told you?" he asked.

Nick nodded. "Last night. I was just wondering what your take on it was."

"You mean, do I believe that Alyssa has psychic visions that foretell the future?" Clay frowned thoughtfully. "I'm not sure what I think about Alyssa's visions. I will tell you this, I know there are times she sees things, knows things that have no other rationalization."

He moved from the top of the table to the chair facing Nick's. "I don't know how much of the story you've heard, but a couple of months ago our friendly banker broke into my parents' house, hit my father over the head, drugged my mother and carried her out to his car in her bedspread. He came back inside, put a new bedspread on the bed in the exact style and pattern, packed a suitcase full of her clothes and personal items, then left.''

Although Nick had heard that Clay's mother had been kidnapped, he hadn't heard the details of the case. "So, the friendly banker wanted it to look as if your mother hit your father, then packed up and fled.''

"Exactly. Meanwhile, while my mother was missing, Alyssa kept having visions of her sitting in her bed. At the time she told me about the vision, I dismissed it. We all knew Mom wasn't in her own bed in her bedroom. She was gone.''

Nick looked at Clay expectantly. He knew there was a reason Clay was telling him all this and he waited patiently to find out what it was.

"We found Mom in a basement decorated to look exactly like her bedroom. Alyssa's vision that made no sense before we found Mom suddenly made complete sense after we found her.'' Clay sighed. "I can give you a dozen times when Alyssa's visions have been right on the money. I can also give you a dozen times when what she saw never came to pass. I'll tell you this…I'm a big enough believer that I never discount what she sees, but I take it all with a tiny grain of salt.''

Nick nodded. "Thanks, Clay. I just wanted to get your input. Now, get home to that beautiful wife of yours.''

"See you tomorrow,'' Clay said.

Nick watched him leave the room, fighting the impulse to call him back and ask him more questions about Alyssa. But the questions he wanted answered had little to do with her visions and more to do with the private areas of her life.

All day long she'd been in his thoughts. It had been impossible for him to dismiss from his mind the taste of her lips, the acquiescence in her response for just a moment.

And it had been impossible for him to forget that moment when she'd violently jerked away from him. What he'd seen in her eyes hadn't been revulsion or disapproval about the kiss.

What he had seen in those lovely, dark eyes of hers had been fear…sheer terror, and he wondered what she hadn't told him.

But he hadn't seen her that morning. He'd gotten up later than usual and had headed directly to the station.

He packed up his briefcase and left the police station. His plan was to linger over dinner at Ruby's until it was almost time for Alyssa to close down the ice-cream parlor, then he intended to ask her about the kiss and about her unusual response.

Dinner at Ruby's was a meat-loaf special and Ruby's company as he lingered over coffee. The big woman sat next to him, nearly overpowering him with her overly sweet scent, but he found her friendly smile and dancing eyes charming.

"I heard a rumor that you were seen out at Clay's wedding as Alyssa's date," she said.

Nick smiled. "Alyssa would reject the term *date*.

Clay asked her to escort me to the wedding and she reluctantly agreed.''

Ruby shook her head. "Don't know what's wrong with that girl. If I was escorting you anywhere, I'd shout it to the world that it *was* a hot date, and I'd make damn sure it was a hot date!"

Nick laughed. "I get the feeling Alyssa has no interest in hot dates."

"That girl spends all her time taking care of strangers and never takes care of herself. That place of hers is eating her alive and she doesn't even realize it. I've offered half a dozen times to buy her out." Ruby's eyes twinkled. "I figured I could tell guests that the place was originally my great-grandmother's bordello. The place would be packed year-round."

Nick grinned. "Ah, not only does the heart of a romantic beat in your chest, but also the heart of a true businesswoman."

"That's me." Ruby studied him for a long moment. "I know you're only in town for as long as it takes to catch the creep that's killing men around here, but it wouldn't hurt if you'd take that time and be a little nice to Alyssa. She's a good woman who isn't always treated nice."

"You mean because of her visions?"

"Ah, so you know the truth about her. She has the gift of the sight, but there are some dumb folks around here who don't see it as a gift, they don't understand that Alyssa is special."

Nick knew she was special, but it had little to do with her visions. The moment he'd tasted her lips, he'd known she was special. She'd stirred him to life again when he'd believed nobody would ever be able to do that again.

"You're a wise woman, Ruby," he replied. "And I think it's time I get across the way and settle in for the night." He looked at his watch. It was eight-thirty and he knew Alyssa shut down the ice-cream shop at nine.

Talking about her, thinking about that all-too-brief kiss they had shared made him want to be with her...to just sit and watch as she finished up her nightly duties.

He rose from the table, as did Ruby. "As usual, another wonderful meal," he said as they approached the cash register.

"You're easy to please," Ruby replied as she took his money. "I suppose I'll see you tomorrow night." She handed him his change.

He nodded. "Good night Ruby."

The night air was hot and dry. He yanked off the tie he'd worn that morning and shoved it into his slacks pocket, then opened the top two buttons of his short-sleeved white shirt.

Instead of walking around the center square, he cut through the parklike setting. Was it here, in the darkness of the large trees and on shadowy park benches, that the murderer met his victims, then lured them to the public areas where they would be killed and left on display?

He couldn't seem to get a handle on the killer. He couldn't figure out why those particular victims, how the perp got the victims to their death places and why the victims were stripped naked.

Just ahead, the lights of the ice-cream parlor pierced through the purple twilight of coming night. At the moment, it seemed more important that he get a handle on Alyssa and find out why a kiss from him had stirred such terror in her.

Chapter 6

The bell tinkled above the door and even with her back to it, Alyssa knew it was Nick who had entered. She wasn't sure how she knew, but she did.

When she turned around he was headed toward the counter, his eyes gleaming with intent that bode ill for her. "We need to talk," he said as he slid onto a stool.

She didn't even attempt to pretend she didn't know what he'd want to talk to her about. "I've got customers," she replied, grateful that there were two families still seated at tables.

"I'll wait. Why don't you get me one of those brownie delights while I'm waiting."

She turned and began to make the dessert for him, trying to slow her heartbeat, which had begun to race from the moment she saw him.

She'd been grateful that morning when he hadn't appeared in the kitchen or dining room. She hadn't wanted to face him, she hadn't been ready to face him.

The night had been spent tossing and turning, playing and replaying that kiss that had touched her lips, but had warmed her to her soul. Along with the memory of the kiss had been the tortured thoughts of the vision.

As the day had gone on, it had become more and more difficult for her to separate the two, the sheer pleasure of the kiss and the utter horror of the vision.

She finished making the brownie delight and turned back to serve him. She didn't want to have the conversation she suspected he intended to have with her. She'd rather just forget the kiss altogether.

"You look tired," he said.

"I am." She grabbed a damp dishcloth and wiped down the counter.

"Ruby told me she thinks this place is eating you alive."

She smiled. "Ruby is a sweetheart and she would love for me to sell to her."

"She mentioned that, said she'd advertise it as her great-grandmother's brothel and it would be full to capacity year-round."

Despite her desire to be cool and aloof, Alyssa couldn't help but laugh. "That's Ruby...always looking at the bottom line."

"What's her story anyway?" Nick dived into his ice cream with a spoon. "She ever been married?"

Alyssa felt herself relaxing somewhat. At least he wasn't asking her about last night. "Rumor has it that years ago Ruby was dating a wealthy young man from Texas. She was madly in love with him, thought they were serious until he officially became engaged to some Texas socialite. It broke her heart and she decided she'd make sure she never needed a man in her life again. It was at that time Ruby set out to be the most successful entrepreneur in the state of Oklahoma."

"Has she succeeded?" Nick licked his spoon and Alyssa remembered the flick of his tongue against hers. She turned to rinse out her dishcloth, giving herself a moment to erase the sensation from her mind.

"I don't know about the entire state of Oklahoma, but rumor has it that Ruby is the second wealthiest person in Cherokee Corners. She owns a lot of land and has interest in half the businesses around the square. I'd say she's done quite well for herself." She turned back to face him as one of the families left the parlor, leaving only one other group between herself and a more serious conversation with Nick.

"I've heard it's a woman thing…the idea that the best revenge for a broken heart is being successful or marrying successfully."

"I wouldn't know. I've never had a broken heart," she replied. As soon as she said it, she realized what a sad commentary it was on her life…that she had reached the ripe old age of twenty-nine and had never had her heart broken.

"Really?" A dark eyebrow lifted upward as he

gazed at her in surprise. "I thought everyone had a heartbreak or two beneath their belts."

"Not me." She wanted to grab her dishcloth again, find something to do instead of stand in front of him with his curiosity lighting his eyes. "My heart has had a few bumps and bruises, but nothing so devastating as total heartbreak."

She watched as the last group of customers left the shop. Somehow she knew the conversation was going to get tougher. "I don't know what you want to discuss with me, but I'm going to be a few minutes here closing up. Maybe we could talk in the morning." If she could put him off until morning, then she knew she could probably get out of the conversation altogether.

"I don't mind waiting. In fact, I can help." He got off the stool and walked to the front door. He turned the Open sign to Closed, then locked the door.

She sighed in defeat. "The best way you can help is just stay out of my way and let me take care of things." Her stomach muscles clenched as she cleaned up the last of the dishes in the large sink, turned off a variety of machines and cleaned off the tables.

As she worked, Nick stood silently watching her, and her tension grew to mammoth proportions. She'd hoped they wouldn't have to talk about the kiss and her violent reaction to it. She'd hoped he'd just write her off as a frigid, uptight woman who didn't like kisses.

But she should have known better, especially since

she'd shared with him the fact that she had visions. There was no way to avoid answering the questions he'd have for her. She just needed to come up with some logical answers rather than telling him about the vision that frightened her more than all others.

Finally, there was nothing left for her to do…nothing but turn and face Nick. "Nick, if this is about last night…about kissing me—" She flushed and broke off.

"Can we go someplace else to talk?" he asked. "Someplace where I don't feel like the whole town is watching us." He gestured toward the windows. With the night-lights on inside the store and the darkness outside the window, she knew he was right. Anyone standing outside would be able to see them easily.

"You want to come up to my room?" he asked.

"No! No, we'll go to my room." In all her visions they were making love in the blue bedroom. That was the very last place she wanted to go with him.

She unlocked her door and opened it wide to allow him into her private quarters. The living area was small, with a kitchenette along one wall. The doors to the tiny bedroom and the bathroom were closed.

"Please, sit down." She gestured him toward the beige sofa decorated with colorful throw pillows. "Would you like a cup of tea? I'm making a cup for myself. Or maybe a soda or something?"

"Sure, tea sounds good." He sat on the sofa and she went to the stove and put water on to boil, her nerves still knotted up in her stomach.

"I've got chamomile, lemon, lavender or regular."

"I like my coffee to taste like coffee and my tea to taste like tea. Regular, please."

As she waited for the water to boil, she watched Nick get up from the sofa and walk over to a bookshelf where she had books and knickknacks and intricate woven baskets.

"These are beautiful," he said, indicating one of the baskets with a colorful design woven into the sides.

"Thanks. My grandmother made them," she said. "She was a master at weaving. She supported herself by selling the baskets around the country. She tried to teach me, but I was always too fumble-fingered."

"I'm sure it takes a special skill to do work this beautiful," he replied.

She finished fixing the tea and carried the two cups and cream and sugar on a tray to the coffee table. He joined her and they both sat on the sofa.

"Dorrie was into Indian art, pottery and baskets…stuff like that. She got interested in it when we moved from Chicago to Oklahoma."

Alyssa was surprised by how easily he spoke of his murdered wife…as if he'd made peace with his loss. "Tell me more about her," she said softly. "How did you meet?"

"Mutual friends. It was a kind of blind-date thing. I didn't want to go and later I found out that she didn't want to go, either." The blue of his eyes was soft with pleasant memories and he set his cup of tea on the tray and leaned back against the colorful pillows.

"The moment I met her I couldn't understand why somebody hadn't already snapped her up. She was beautiful, bright and funny. She worked as an E.R. nurse, so she understood the meaning of stress, and at the time that I met her I was definitely under stress."

His eyes darkened to the deep blue of fiery gas flames. He drew a deep breath and sat forward to pick up his cup of tea once again. He took a sip, then another as Alyssa struggled to find something to say.

But apparently he refused to go the direction his thoughts were attempting to take him, a place that had caused the deepening, troubling hue of his eyes.

"You know, I've never really understood why people who lose spouses often swear off the entire institution of marriage," he said.

"Maybe if they had a really bad marriage they don't want to take the chance of repeating it," Alyssa replied. "They're afraid of trying once again."

"In this day and age if you have a really bad marriage you don't have to wait for a spouse to die to get out of it."

She nodded. "True, but maybe if you have a really great marriage and lose your spouse, you're afraid you'll never experience the same thing again."

"You won't experience the exact same thing," he agreed easily. "Different women, different relationships, but that doesn't mean a second marriage can't be just as wonderful as the first."

"I can't believe I'm hearing a man extol the virtues of marriage," she said teasingly.

His gaze warmed her as he smiled, that sexy half smile that evoked a seductive wave of pleasure inside her. "I loved Dorrie, but in the time we had together I also realized I loved being married."

He took another sip of his tea then continued, "I liked being half of a whole, fighting over the last piece of pie, compromising on important issues. I liked having the same person in bed with me night after night, sharing every part of myself, both physically and emotionally with another. So, what scared you last night when I kissed you?"

Alyssa had been lulled by the conversation, and the abruptness of his question caught her completely unprepared even though she'd known eventually it would come up.

She broke eye contact with him and stared at her cup, still sitting on the tray. "I wasn't scared...I just didn't like your kiss." She reached a hand up to grasp the ends of a strand of her hair.

"Alyssa..." His voice was soft, almost cajoling, and she looked up to meet his soft blue gaze once again. "I'm a specially trained FBI agent. That means I have a sort of built-in lie detector. It wasn't revulsion or disgust that I saw in your eyes when you ran away from me last night. It was fear...terror, and I want to know what's going on."

He reached out and took the strand of her hair from her fingers. "Talk to me, Alyssa."

For the first time, she realized she had to tell him. She'd thought that by not speaking of it at all, she'd somehow keep the vision from coming true. She now realized that knowledge meant power. If he knew about the vision, then he could be an active participant in making sure that it didn't come true.

She started to reach up for her hair once again, but he captured her hand and held it tight. She drew a deep breath. "I saw you in a recurring vision for about a month before you actually arrived here in Cherokee Corners."

His eyes grew slightly darker and he scooted closer to her, still holding her hand. "Are you sure it was me?"

"Positive. I saw your face…your blue eyes and dark hair, your strong jawline and stubborn chin."

"Determined, not stubborn," he corrected her with a half smile. But the smile lasted only a moment. "What was I doing in this vision of yours?"

Although she'd thought herself prepared to tell him all about the vision, she quickly realized she hadn't quite prepared herself for sharing the intimate details. The heat of a blush clawed its way up her neck and swept into her cheeks.

"By the blush on your face, I think I might like this vision," he said.

She pulled her hand from his and stood, needing some distance from his body warmth, from his scent, as she spoke of the vision.

"When it begins, we're making love in the bed in the room where you're staying." As she spoke the words, the sensations from the vision filled her.

Her nipples grew taut, as if his hands were stroking

her there. A whispered heat slid down the side of her neck, as if his lips were tasting the skin just beneath her earlobe.

"We're making love on the blue sheets, and it's passionate…sensual…fevered…and then I stab you to death."

Nick blinked as if startled out of a pleasant daydream. "You stab me?" He raked a hand through his hair. "I like to think when I make love to a woman I inspire great emotion, but that's not exactly the reaction I had in mind."

"It's not funny, Nick," she exclaimed, and to her horror the burn of hot tears stung her eyes. "It's awful and horrible and the night you walked in here I felt the worst kind of terror I've ever felt."

The tears that had burned in her eyes now scalded her cheeks as they fell. There was no way she could make him understand the horror the vision shot through her each time she experienced it.

He was up and off the couch in a single, graceful movement. He pulled her into his arms and held her with her cheek pressed tightly against his shirt. "You're right, it isn't funny. Anything that makes you cry isn't funny at all." He stroked her hair and his sweet words released the dam of emotions she'd kept inside far too long.

Deep, wrenching sobs racked her. Nick didn't try to talk to her, nor did he do anything in an attempt to stop her tears. He did the only thing she needed at the moment.

He held her while she cried.

As her tears flowed, she realized not only was she crying from the trauma of the vision about Nick that she had endured for the past month, she was also weeping stored-up tears from the kidnapping and recovery of her aunt Rita. She was also crying for a lifetime that so far had been filled with far too much isolation and loneliness. She wept for herself and she wept for Nick, who had loved so deeply and had lost his wife to a horrible death.

Finally, the sobs halted and she raised her face from Nick's pleasant-smelling shirt and looked into too-blue eyes that nearly stole her breath away.

In an instant she was aware of the strength of his chest against her softer breasts, the heat of his hands as he swept one over her hair and the other up and down her back. She could feel the solidity of his thighs and something else…the hardness of his arousal against her.

She swiped at her eyes and stepped out of the embrace, fighting against the heady, sweeping thrill that enfolded her as she realized his response to her closeness.

"I'm sorry," she said awkwardly. "I didn't mean to fall apart."

"I apologize for making light of your vision," he replied. "Come, sit down and let's talk about it." He showed no overt signs of whatever desire had made his physical response.

Together they returned to the sofa and sat side by side. Alyssa picked up her cup of tea, which was now cold, but she sipped it in an effort to regain her complete composure.

"Now, tell me again about every detail of this particular vision." He must have seen the pained look on her face and he smiled gently. "You don't have to tell me the sexual details, you can skip over them."

Relief flowed through her. "There's really not a lot to tell. Like I said before, when the vision first begins we're in bed making love, then the scene shifts and we're beneath a strange, misshapen tree." She frowned, concentrating on the memory of the tree. Why did it seem so familiar? Where had she seen it before?

"And that's where you stab me?"

She nodded, fighting against the wave of despair that swept through her. "I use a long, sharp knife and I plunge it into you over and over again...I see blood...blood everywhere, then the scene goes black."

She didn't tell him the worst part of the vision, about the heady surge of power that had shot through her as she stabbed him. She didn't mention the almost Godlike omnipotent feeling that had rushed through her. That was the most horrid part of all about the vision.

"Alyssa." For the second time that night Nick took her hand in his. "Can you think of anything or anyone who could drive you to kill them? Can you think of any reason that would prompt you to pick up a knife and stab somebody to death?"

"Of course not," she answered without hesitation. "I'm not a killer. I could never take anyone's life."

"Then, what are you frightened of?" he asked softly.

What was she frightened of? So many thoughts flew into her head, thoughts she couldn't share with him, thoughts she had never shared with anyone.

She was afraid that if she continued working the bed-and-breakfast, it would eat her alive, and yet she was afraid if she stopped working there she would have nothing else in her life.

She was afraid to get too close to anyone, certain that her visions would eventually drive them away, afraid that she would love and finally have her heart broken and never recover from the experience.

"I don't know," she finally replied. "I'm afraid that even though I don't think I'm capable of hurting anyone, something might change and make me harm you. That's why I tried to be unfriendly to you, to keep you at arm's distance since you arrived. The vision is so vivid each time it comes and it's usually the ones that are vivid that eventually come true."

He squeezed her hand more tightly and she felt the warmth steal up her arm and right to the center of her chest. "I think there's only one way to show you that this particular vision isn't going to come true."

"What's that?" she asked.

His eyes glittered teasingly, but beneath the teasing light she saw the flames of something quite different. "I think I should take you upstairs to the blue bedroom and make mad, passionate love to you. I can promise that you will be positively unable to stab me to death, because you'll be limp with pleasure.''

Despite her worries, a small burst of laughter left her, even as a swirling fire claimed the center of her being. ''You're pretty sure of yourself. What happens if I'm not limp with pleasure, but rather unfulfilled and angry?''

He took a finger and slowly traced it down the side of her cheek, then moved it achingly slow over the fullness of her lips. ''I can promise you that won't happen.''

She was frozen, held captive by his touch, unable to move as his finger continued to smooth over the curves of her mouth.

Alyssa certainly wasn't a virgin. Two years before, she'd had a brief relationship. It had lasted only three weeks and they had parted as friends and remained close still.

But nothing she'd experienced in those three weeks of their lovemaking had prepared her for her turbulent response to Nick's simplest touch.

Her stomach quivered and she felt as if every nerve ending in her body was on fire. She wanted to draw his finger into her mouth and taste him.

She wanted to wrap her arms around his neck and press herself intimately against him, feel the hard length of his desire seeking entrance into the very depths of her.

''Or, we can make love right here, then move up to my bed and have a repeat performance,'' he whispered as he leaned into her. His mouth scorched hers, breathing fire through her as his tongue entered her mouth.

She gave herself to the kiss, her tongue battling with his as her arms wrapped around his neck. In the back of her mind she thought that if he made love as well as he kissed, then no woman had ever been left unfulfilled by Nick Mead.

He eased her onto her back on the sofa, using one hand to spill the colorful decorative pillows to the floor. His mouth never left hers as he lay half across her body and half off. The part of him that weighed on her felt heavenly…so warm and masculine.

His lips finally left hers, but only to blaze a trail of fire just beneath her ear and down the length of her throat. She couldn't help the soft moan that issued from her as one of his hands moved across her stomach, then up to smooth over one breast, then the other.

Even through the material of her thin cotton dress and bra, her nipples responded to his touch, pebbling to rock hardness.

He raised his head to look at her, his eyes gleaming like twin sapphires. ''I want you, Alyssa. I've wanted you from the moment I walked into the ice-cream parlor and saw you staring at me.''

''And I wanted you before I even met you, when you were just a vision in my mind and nothing more,'' she replied, her voice deeper than usual and throaty with desire.

Once again his mouth stole over hers, hungrily taking possession not only of her lips, but her spinning senses, as well.

At the moment, the terror of her vision seemed very far away and the only thing important was the taste of Nick's mouth, the hot flames he stroked into her as his hand moved across her breasts.

Bang. Bang. Bang.

It took her a moment to realize the sound she heard was not the crashing of her heartbeat, but rather a knock on her door.

Nick groaned and pulled his mouth from hers. "Do you have to answer it?" he asked softly.

"I do."

"Are you sure?"

Despite the desire that rocketed through her, she laughed softly. "Unfortunately, I'm sure."

Reluctantly he sat up and pulled her to a sitting position beside him. He raked a hand through his hair and expelled a deep breath that was obviously one of frustration.

"Just a minute," Alyssa called out. She needed a minute to get herself under control, to halt the racing of her pulse, to make the transition from desire to duty. She stood, her legs feeling rubbery and her body temperature so heated she felt feverish.

She opened her door to see Michael Stanmeyer standing in the darkened hallway. "Michael...come in."

The bald, tall, thin man slid through the doorway like a wraith unsure of its welcome. When he saw Nick his brown eyes widened slightly and he shuffled backward as if to leave the room. "You're busy...I can come back later."

"Nonsense." Alyssa grabbed one of his thin arms and half propelled him toward Nick. "Nick, I don't believe you've met Michael. Michael, this is Nick. He's staying in the blue room." Nick stood.

Michael nodded, his gaze not on Nick but rather on the floor. He didn't offer his hand for a shake. "Nice to meet you," he mumbled.

"Nice to meet you, too," Nick replied.

Alyssa saw Nick's sharp gaze taking in every detail of her boarder. "What do you need, Michael?" she asked.

"Towels. I'm sorry to be a bother, but I'd like some clean towels."

"I'll get them for you." She left him standing awkwardly in the center of the living room as she went into the bathroom to retrieve a couple of clean towels for him.

It was obvious when she returned from the bathroom that neither man had spoken in the brief moments while she'd been gone. Michael stood looking down at the floor and the only change in Nick was that he had sat down.

She handed Michael the towels, he murmured thanks, then raced toward the door and disappeared back into the darkened hallway.

"What's his story?" Nick asked the moment Alyssa had closed the door once again.

She didn't return to the sofa to sit next to him. Although she still felt the residual effects of Nick's kisses, his caresses, the mood that had overtaken her earlier had vanished and she wasn't prepared for a repeat.

"I'm not sure what his story is," she replied. "I think he's on some sort of disability and is painfully shy. I can tell you this, he keeps his room immaculate, never causes problems and always pays on time. Why?"

Nick's eyes were dark...thoughtful. "He fits the tentative physical profile of the killer we've come up with."

Alyssa stared at him in surprise. "Physical profile?"

"From what little evidence we have to go on, we think the murderer is tall and very thin. A bald head would explain why we never have found any hair evidence on any of the bodies."

"Michael wouldn't hurt a flea," Alyssa said, but even as she said it she thought about the fact that although Michael had been staying here nearly two years she knew virtually nothing about the man or his past.

Nick stood and walked over to her. He placed his hands on her shoulders and gazed at her intently. "From now on I don't want you to allow him in here when you're alone. I don't care if he wants towels, a bar of soap or a freshly baked cookie."

"I'm not in danger, Nick," she protested. "The victims have all been men."

"So far." He dropped his hands from her shoulders and sighed deeply. "We don't have a handle on this guy yet. We don't know if he may change his victim

profile, start killing women or children. Just indulge
me in this.''

"Okay," she agreed uneasily.

"We have unfinished business between us, but you
look tired and I think what you need more than anything is a good night's sleep. Go to bed, Alyssa, and
have sweet dreams.''

"I am tired," she admitted. The night of emotion
had left her wrung out.

He smiled, that teasing, sexy smile, then leaned forward and kissed her on the forehead, a lingering kiss
that whispered of heat. "Good night," he said, then
slipped out her door.

For a long moment she stood, waiting for the
warmth of his kiss to pass, and when it did, a chill
swept through her as she remembered his warning
about Michael Stanmeyer. Was it possible, for the
past two years, she'd had a serial killer living under
her roof?

Chapter 7

The task-force room was beginning to look and smell like the back lot of a fast-food restaurant. The trash bin overflowed with hamburger wrappers and oil-soaked French-fry boxes. A half-eaten pizza sat in a box on one of the tables, along with the remnants of a fried catfish meal one of the men had ordered the day before.

Although Nick was aware that the room was trashed, at the moment he had other, more important things on his mind as he listened to each of the men give updates on the work they had accomplished since the day before.

He was pleased by how much they had accomplished. Family and friends of victims had been reinterviewed, records had been checked and rechecked. It was obvious that all the members of the task team were making this the number one priority in their lives…as it should be until they caught the killer.

The only person who had not been reinterviewed was Virginia Maxwell, and Nick told the others that he'd take care of it since the woman was staying at the Redbud Bed-and-Breakfast.

"Okay, so to recap what we have. We've got four victims. Gregory Maxwell, age thirty-two…Sam McClane, age thirty-five, Tim O'Brien, age thirty-eight and Jonathon Blackbird, who was thirty-three," Nick recapped. "Gregory Maxwell's marriage appeared to be stable, both Sam and Tim had reputations for being wanderers despite their marriages, and Jonathon was single. They were all found stabbed, then stripped naked and left at some point or other in the square. None of them seemed to be having financial difficulty and none of their family members can state that any of them had any real enemies."

"Except we know that Billy Thunder threatened both Sam and Tim in the weeks prior to their deaths," Clay interjected.

Nick frowned. "I don't remember seeing that in any of my reports."

"If I remember right, Jason Sheller took the initial reports about that, but I don't know if he did any follow-up or not." It was obvious from Clay's tone that he didn't particularly care for Sheller.

In the time Nick had been working out of the Cherokee Corners Police Department, he'd found the young, good-looking officer to be a pest, constantly trying to intrude into the task-force work.

"Clay, do you have Billy Thunder's address? I'll try to interview him this evening."

Clay hesitated a moment, then nodded. "I'll give you his address, but you might want to take Alyssa with you. His place is difficult to find even with directions and Billy isn't exactly the friendly sort, but he and Alyssa are good friends."

Alyssa. Nick had consciously tried to keep thoughts of her out of his head, but now that Clay had mentioned her name, Nick's head was filled with her.

As the others continued to discuss the cases, Nick couldn't help but remember last night and those moments when Alyssa had been in his arms.

He'd been shocked by the vision she'd been having of him, but had believed her when she'd told him about it. He didn't pretend to understand where the vision came from or what it could possibly mean.

What he did know was that on the first night he had walked into the ice-cream parlor, she'd looked as if she'd seen a ghost. He also knew that no matter what her vision presented to her, there was no way he would ever believe that she could intentionally harm him or anyone else.

But it wasn't her telling him about the vision that had made him consciously keep her out of his mind. It had been the scent of her that he'd tried to forget while he focused on work. It had been the taste of her lips he'd needed to forget so he could keep his concentration where it belonged.

It had been the feel of her soft, silky skin and her feminine curves against his hard body he'd shoved to the back of his mind so he could keep his attention on trying to catch a killer.

The mere sound of her name brought it all back to him...the fast flutter of her heart against his own, the taut nipples beneath his fingertips, the ravenous hunger that had whipped through him for more...and more.

They would have made love right there on her sofa if it hadn't been for the interruption. This thought brought him back to the here and now and the job at hand.

"Does anyone here know anything about Michael Stanmeyer?" he asked.

"I've seen him around a couple of times, usually at night." Simon frowned thoughtfully. "He's tall and skinny as a rail and strange, but I don't know anything about his background, what he does for a living...nothing. I'll check him out."

"Good. And anyone else that you think fits the physical profile we've come up with should be checked out, as well. Simon and John, you know the people in town. Anyone you can think of off the top of your head that would be tall and thin?"

Simon and John exchanged glances with one another. "We'll have to think on it a bit," John said. "We'll make a list and spend the afternoon doing some questioning, checking out alibis for the murders."

"Good. Bud, why don't you and Tony spend the afternoon on the computers. I want to know if any similar crimes have taken place anywhere in the country.'' He turned his attention to Clay. ''Anything you can do to hurry up the lab results from Jonathon Blackbird's murder?''

''I can make some phone calls, ruffle some feathers and see what we can get back from the lab in Oklahoma City.''

Nick knew as an FBI agent he would be able to step on more toes, pull more weight than Clay, but he also knew it was important to maintain certain job delineation within the task force, and Clay's specialty was forensic evidence.

''Whoever killed these men knew them personally. This is no stranger crime. I don't believe the victims were chosen by sheer opportunity.'' Nick paused a moment to gather his thoughts. ''I could be wrong, but there's a level of rage here that makes me believe these victims have been specifically chosen. All we have to figure out is what the damn connection is between these men and the killer.''

''We're working on it, boss,'' Bud said.

''I know. And you all have work to do now, so get out of here and we'll meet again at seven in the morning.''

He waited until all the others had left the room, then walked over to the large corkboard decorated with crime scene photographs. It was a grisly display of the ugliness of unnatural death. The four men in the prime of their lives, stabbed multiple times in the chest and left naked in the square.

Nick's job was to crawl into the skin, get into the mind of the killer. It had always been a job he did well. Even with the elusive Murphy, Nick had understood the man and his killings. He had known the kind of man and the background that had created that particular monster. But this killer remained elusive to Nick.

He turned from the board and began a little janitorial duty. He threw away plastic and foam cups along with the remnants of too many lunches and dinners eaten in the room. He'd just tied up the large garbage bag in the trash bin, when Glen Cleburg walked in.

"I told you I'd be happy to have our janitor take care of this room, too," he said as Nick pulled the bag from the container.

"I know, and I appreciate the offer." Nick gestured toward the bulletin board and the corkboard. "But some of the material we have up here is sensitive. I'd rather take care of the trash myself and limit the people who have access to this room." At the moment there were only three people who had keys to the task-force room. Nick, Clay and Chief Cleberg.

"Any breaks?" An anxious furrow indented Glen's forehead.

Nick wished he had something positive to give the man who was responsible for the safety of the people of Cherokee Corners. Unfortunately, he didn't. "These things take time, Chief Cleberg."

"I know…I know." The furrow across his forehead cut even deeper. "But if the killer stays true to the time line of the last four murders, we're getting ready for another one to happen, aren't we? There's been about three weeks between each murder.''

"We're doing everything in our power to see that another one doesn't happen."

"I'm trying to keep extra patrols around the square, but we're a small department and I can't leave the rest of the town without police presence on the off chance we'll be at the right place at exactly the right time to stop a killer." Cleberg sighed in frustration.

"I know you're doing what you can," Nick said.

"Things would be easier if it wasn't the height of the tourist season," Cleberg continued. "We've got too many strangers, folks who are as much at risk as all the rest of us."

"There's one other thing you can do for me," Nick said.

"What's that?"

"I'd like a list of any police officers who have quit for any reason or been fired in the past two years. I'd also like a complete roster of all the people currently working for the police department."

Glen's eyes widened. "Surely you don't think a cop is responsible for these murders?"

"At this point we aren't ruling out anyone," Nick replied.

"But what makes you think there's any kind of cop connection to all this?"

"Nothing specific except that the killer seems to be particularly good at not leaving behind much forensic evidence, and that makes me think the killer knows more than an ordinary person about trace evidence and transfer.''

Nick had thought it impossible for Glen's frown to get any deeper, but it did as grim lines bracketed his mouth. ''I'll have a list ready for you first thing in the morning.''

Glen left and Nick followed. He locked up the room, then carried the bag of garbage out the back door to the Dumpster. It was just after three but his day was far from over. He intended to reinterview Virginia Maxwell, then see if Alyssa would take him to Billy Thunder's house for an interview.

Alyssa. He'd consciously fought to keep thoughts of her at bay all day, but as he got into his car and headed for the inn, his mind exploded with sensory memories of her in his arms.

However, it wasn't just the physical pleasures that swept through him once again, but an emotional reaction, as well. Somehow, in telling him about her vision, she'd opened herself to him.

When she'd wept in his arms, he'd felt a level of trust emanating from her, and later as they'd kissed, as she'd allowed him to hold her, to caress her, he'd felt the utter openness, her complete vulnerability to him.

It had both frightened him and thrilled him at the same time. It had been three years since he'd felt a woman open herself to him not only physically, but mentally and emotionally, as well.

But he didn't know what the future held, where his quest for Murphy might eventually take him and what price Alyssa might have to pay emotionally before the serial killer haunting her town was caught. He couldn't forget that the last woman he'd been close to had wound up dead.

Alyssa was in the green bedroom changing the bedding. The couple from Kansas City, Cindy and Dave, had checked out and new guests would be arriving the next morning.

Even though she had her back to the doorway, she felt Nick's presence. His expensive cologne, coupled with the clean, masculine scent of him, filled the air, and every nerve ending in her body went on high alert. She turned to see him standing in the doorway.

"Goofing off in the middle of the day, Agent Mead?" she asked. It was amazing to her that she now felt so at ease with him, that by sharing the secrets of her vision with him and hearing his calm assurances, she felt more uninhibited with him than she'd ever felt with anyone else.

"You'd better stop looking at me that way or you're going to have to change those sheets all over again when I get finished with you."

She laughed, slightly breathless at the blatant sexual warning in his voice. "And just how am I looking at you?"

He took a step into the room. "Your eyes are flirting with me, propositioning me and trying to cajole me into bed." That sexy half smile curved his lips. "Unfortunately I can't take you up on your offer at the moment. I'll have to fit you into my schedule later.''

She threw a pillow at him. He caught it and tossed it back to her with a laugh. ''What makes you think I want you to work me into your schedule?'' she replied with mock indignation. ''I've got my own schedule to adhere to.''

His teasing smile fell away. ''Actually, I was wondering if maybe later you could work me into your schedule.''

She could tell by his expression that he wasn't teasing anymore. ''What do you need?'' she asked.

''I've got to interview Billy Thunder, and Clay recommended I take you with me. So, could you get somebody to cover you here for an hour or so later this afternoon?''

''Why do you want to interview Billy?'' she asked, surprised by the loyalty, the defensiveness that arose as she thought of the man who had been her first and only lover, a man she still considered a dear friend.

''I just need to talk to him,'' Nick said, obviously being vague on purpose.

''It will take me a little while to get somebody to cover things here.''

''That's all right. I've got to reinterview Virginia. Is she here?''

''I think she's in her room. This is usually about the time of day she takes a nap.''

''Well, I'm going to have to interrupt her nap. I'll check in with you later and see what time will work for you to take me to Billy's place.''

Nick disappeared from the doorway and she heard him knock on Virginia's door.

Michael Stanmeyer's door was closed, as well, as it was most of the time. Alyssa couldn't remember the last time she'd actually been in that room. Michael changed his own bedding and cleaned the room. He was never late with his payments and made few requests. She'd considered him the guest from heaven until last night when Nick had told her that Michael fit the physical profile of the killer.

She'd spent all morning wondering what might possibly be in Michael's room that he didn't want anyone to see. Did he have a knife collection? Bloody clothing? Grisly souvenirs from his kills?

Legally she knew she had the right to enter his room at any time, but she didn't want to peek in until Michael was out, and he rarely left the room before evening.

She finished making the bed, then cleaned the rest of the room and the bathroom. When she was done, Nick was still inside Virginia's room.

Alyssa went back downstairs and contacted Mary to see if she could come in and work for a couple of hours. Mary agreed to come within the next hour. Alyssa poured herself a glass of lemonade and carried it out on the veranda to wait for Mary to arrive and for Nick to finish speaking with Virginia.

The sun beat down with relentless intensity but the shade on the veranda made sitting there bearable. She sipped her lemonade and thought about Billy and why Nick might want to talk to him.

Billy's temper was legendary around town, but he wasn't a killer. If Nick thought he was on a hot trail, then he was going to be disappointed.

She took another sip of her cold drink and leaned her head against the high back of the wicker chair. She'd slept better last night than she had in years.

It was as if in telling Nick about the vision that had haunted her, some of the burden, the terror, the turmoil inside her had been released.

She and Nick were going to make love. It was as inevitable as the sun going down in the west and rising once again in the east. It had been inevitable from the moment he had walked into her establishment.

Beneath the fear of his appearance, despite the horror of his actual presence after a month of having visions about him, there had been a thrill of anticipation. In that single instance of seeing him for the first time, she'd known him intimately, as a woman knows a man she's made love to.

Every day, every moment that she'd been near him, her body had sung with the need to experience in reality what she'd experienced only in her mind.

She had no illusions about any kind of a long-term relationship with Nick. He was in town to do a job, and once that job was done, he'd return to his life in Tulsa.

But she knew what her future held, and it was a future of being alone. She'd long ago made peace with that fact.

"You look relaxed," Nick said as he stepped out onto the veranda.

She looked up at him. "And you look tense," she replied. It was true. His jaw muscles were bunched and a frown line creased his forehead.

He drew a deep breath and released it slowly, his jaw relaxing and the line disappearing. He sank into the chair next to her. "Talking to Virginia Maxwell is an experience."

Alyssa smiled. "She can be exhausting. But I feel so sorry for her. I can't imagine loving somebody, sharing a life with him, then losing him to a murder. I'd think it would be easier never to love." She suddenly realized what she'd said and she drew a hand to her mouth in dismay. "Oh, Nick, I'm sorry. That was insensitive of me."

"Don't apologize. It's true, losing somebody like that is horrible, and I think some of Virgina's maniclike energy and demands are maybe part of her grieving process. She needs to feel as if she's in control of her world. Did you find somebody to come help so you can leave with me?"

She blinked to process the rapid change of subject. "Yes, Mary should be here anytime, then we can leave. Billy's place is about a twenty-minute drive from here. It's kind of hard to find."

"I'll drive and you can direct me."

At that moment Mary arrived, and within fifteen minutes they were in Nick's car and headed for Billy's place.

"You're wrong, you know," Nick said as they turned off the main highway and headed south on a dirt road.

"Wrong about what?"

"That it would be easier not to love than to lose somebody. As devastating as Dorrie's death was to me, the real tragedy would have been if I'd missed out on the four years of loving I had with her."

"Who killed her, Nick? And why?" They were questions that had burned inside her since she'd first had the vision of Dorrie and Nick.

She saw him tighten his fingers around the steering wheel and was instantly sorry she'd asked. But when he spoke, his voice was soft and controlled.

"It began five years ago in Chicago. Somebody was killing young women and carving into their chest the letter M. I became obsessed with the case from the moment I was assigned to it. The killer fascinated me. His victims were always the same…young, dark-haired and pretty. They were found in motel rooms, their throats slit and the carving done postmortem."

He turned onto the road she indicated, another dirt road little more than a path, then continued speaking. "The women weren't sexually assaulted in any way and one day I mouthed off to a reporter that it was obvious the killer used his knife instead of his penis to violate the women. The next victim was raped and a taunting note to me was left by the killer."

"Oh, Nick." She reached out and placed a hand on his arm, the muscles rigid beneath her touch.

"My supervisor was thrilled that I'd managed to stir the perp to make personal contact and he encouraged me to continue the dialogue by talking to reporters. After every interview I gave, Murphy, as he called himself, contacted me by letter or by cell-phone calls, which were untraceable. We were hoping he'd give something away in those communications that would lead us to identify and arrest him."

"But he didn't," she said softly and removed her hand from his arm.

Nick shook his head. "No, and in fact, the communications with me seemed to stir him to kill more women, kill faster, and so I was ordered to stop all communication and back off. It was around this time that the possibility of a transfer to Tulsa came up. Dorrie begged me to take the transfer. Somehow she knew I'd gotten too close to this case, this killer. I finally agreed and we moved to Tulsa and I tried to put Murphy behind."

Again Alyssa noticed the white of his knuckles as he gripped the steering wheel and she was sorry she'd asked, sorry to have brought the tragedy back into his mind. "Nick, you don't have to finish if you don't want to," she said.

He flashed her a grim smile. "No, it's all right." His fingers loosened slightly on the wheel. "Anyway, we'd only been in Tulsa for a few months when Dorrie was murdered, compliments of Murphy, and we've never caught him."

"Have you heard from him?"

"No. I never received another note, another phone call, nothing after Dorrie's murder, but that doesn't mean I've stopped looking for him. I've been hunting him for years and won't really rest until he's finally found and put away forever."

"Maybe he's already in prison, or dead," she said. "I mean, since you've never heard from him again, maybe he's already been put away forever."

"Maybe," he agreed, visibly relaxing. "Nowhere in the country has there been any more murders of women with his mark on them. Personally, I hope he's burning in hell as we speak."

"That's what he deserves," she exclaimed, then pointed to a thick wooded area ahead. "There's a road that turns off coming up on the right in the midst of those woods. You need to take it."

He cleared his throat and offered her another smile, this one less grim than the last. "Thanks for coming with me. I would have never found my way out here on my own."

"That's all right. It's kind of nice to be out of the bed-and-breakfast. I've been thinking about what you said last night about Michael Stanmeyer...about him fitting the physical profile of the killer?"

"Yeah?" He slowed the car as the wooded trail they traveled narrowed.

"I just thought I should tell you that I know he often goes out late in the evenings, although I don't know what time he usually returns, and it's been months and months since I've actually been inside his room."

"Really? How did he come to rent from you?"

"He showed up almost two years ago and asked if he could rent a room indefinitely. At the time I'd just sunk the last of my savings into the final renovations and was thrilled to have anyone interested in a room.

From the moment he arrived he's been quiet, unobtrusive and always pays on time. But I suddenly realized I don't know anything about him.''

"I've got one of the men on the task force checking him out, and maybe later tonight if he takes a walk or whatever he does in the evenings, we could peek into his room and see if there's anything amiss. On another subject, I guess Virginia's plans are to eventually leave town?''

"That's what she's told me," Alyssa replied. "She's just waiting for the house to sell. She says she can't think about going back to the home where she and Greg were so happy.''

"Has she said where she's going from here?" Nick asked.

"Not really. I think she has family back East somewhere, and I got the impression she'll go back there.''

They broke out of the wooded area. Billy's house was just ahead, a neat one-story two-bedroom house. On the side of the house was a large, empty corral.

Nick pulled up and parked. Before she could open her car door, he was out of the car.

He took only two steps when an explosion thundered in the air and Alyssa saw the dirt next to Nick's feet kick up.

Nick grabbed a gun from his ankle holster as he scrabbled around the side of the car, putting the vehicle between himself and the house. "Stay in the car," he shouted to Alyssa. "Stay in the car...the crazy bastard just tried to shoot me!''

Chapter 8

Adrenaline spiked through Nick as he watched the house over the top of the back of the car. He saw Alyssa's car door open and her legs swing out. "Stay inside," he commanded. "He tried to kill me."

"If Billy tried to kill you, you'd be dead. He never misses." Ignoring his protests, she got out of the car and stood, a perfect target in her bright red sundress. "Billy. It's me, Alyssa."

"Who's that you got with you?" The deep voice boomed from the shadows of the front door.

"A friend of mine. Somebody who needs to talk to you."

Nick stood, gun at the ready, energy still pumping through him. What in the hell was going on here? Was he here to interview a lunatic?

"Come on, Nick. He won't shoot you if I'm with

you,'' Alyssa said, a lightness in her tone that belied the seriousness of the situation as far as Nick was concerned.

''Who knows what's got him so stirred up today,'' she added more to herself than to him.

As she headed toward the house, Nick hurriedly joined her, falling into step beside her, his gun now lowered but still firmly gripped in his hand.

They were halfway to the porch, when the man appeared out of the shadows. Nick had assumed Billy Thunder was a Native American, but he'd been wrong. The man who stepped out on the porch had shaggy sandy hair, the top of it bleached nearly white from hours in the sun.

He was broad-shouldered, but ripcord lean, and moved with the grace of a wild animal as he came off the porch and met them at the foot of the stairs. ''Who's your friend, Alyssa?'' he asked, his green eyes holding Nick's in a nonverbal confrontation.

''Nick Mead. I'm an FBI agent.'' Nick leaned down and tucked his gun back into the ankle holster. ''I'm here in Cherokee Corners trying to find a murderer.''

''And your investigation has led you to me.'' Billy lowered his gun and sighed. ''Come on inside. We might as well get out of this heat. This shouldn't take long.''

''What are you doing greeting people by shooting at them?'' Alyssa asked as the three of them walked up the stairs to the porch and Billy opened the door that led into the house.

"Some ass wrote <u>Cheri's</u> name and directions to this place in half a dozen truck-stop bathrooms between here and Tulsa. I've had men pulling up looking for a good time all week long."

"Billy, I'm sorry." Alyssa touched his arm, a touch of familiarity that instantly forced an edge of jealousy through Nick.

"Cheri is your wife?" he asked as Billy gestured both he and Alyssa to sit in the neat but barren living room.

"No, my sister. I don't have a wife."

Too bad, Nick thought. He'd much have preferred it if Billy had a drop-dead gorgeous wife in his bed each night.

Nick sat on the sofa, but Alyssa remained standing. "Is she in her room?" she asked Billy. He nodded. "I'll just go visit with her while you two talk."

Billy's gaze was warm on Alyssa and he smiled, a private kind of smile that once again stirred something rather unpleasant in Nick. Jealousy...he couldn't remember the last time he'd felt it, but he recognized that was exactly what he was feeling right now.

Alyssa disappeared down a hallway and Nick took a notepad and pen from his pocket. It was ridiculous for him to be jealous. Alyssa had spent her entire life here. Of course she would have friends...male, as well as female. And some of those men might have at one time or another been lovers. And something about the way Billy and Alyssa had looked at one another made Nick suspect they had been lovers at one time or another.

"I've been wondering how long it was going to take for somebody to get around to talking to me," Billy said. He sat in a chair next to the sofa, an edgy energy radiating from him.

"I can save you a lot of time and trouble. Yes, I threatened Sam McClane and Tim O'Brien...told them both I'd shoot them dead if they continued to come sniffing around my sister. They were both the worst kind of hound dogs, always looking for the weak and defenseless. I threatened them, but I didn't kill either one of them." Billy's eyes met Nick's steadily.

"Do you remember where you were on the night of those murders?"

"I can tell you where I am every night of my life...here with my sister. I never leave her alone."

"Your sister...how old is she?"

"Twenty-two."

"And she can corroborate that you were here on those dates?" Nick asked.

"No."

Nick eyed the man in surprise. "Why not?"

Billy's gaze left Nick's and he raked a hand through his hair as a sigh escaped him. "It would be easier seeing than trying to explain." He stood. "Why don't you come and meet my sister."

Nick followed Billy down the hallway to a closed bedroom door, his curiosity piqued. Billy opened the door and he and Nick entered what appeared to be a little girl's fantasy bedroom.

Nick's first impression was of a pink ruffled fairyland. A canopy bed was covered with stuffed animals, and cartoons played silently on a television that sat on a white desk. White shelves were filled with children's books and girlie toys.

Alyssa and a young woman with long white-blond hair sat on the floor by the window with Barbie dolls in hand. The blonde looked up and Nick's breath caught in his chest at her beauty.

It was a classic beauty. Perfect peaches-and-cream skin and eyes the color of a clear autumn sky. Her mouth was a perfect cupid's bow as she smiled at them. "Look, Billy…Alyssa is playing Barbie with me." There was childlike innocence radiating from her pretty eyes and Nick knew in an instant the burden Billy Thunder must carry on his shoulders.

Alyssa smiled at the two men. "Cheri tells me I play much better than Billy."

Billy snorted, a sound something between indulgence and embarrassment.

"Are you one of Billy's friends?" Cheri asked, looking at Nick.

"Actually, I'm a friend of Alyssa's," Nick replied.

"You're handsome. You want to play with us?" Cheri asked.

"I can't right now. I need to talk some more with your brother," Nick replied. He looked at Billy, and together the two men left and returned to the living room.

"She was oxygen deprived at birth," Billy said before Nick could ask. "As you can tell, she's beautiful but will never have anything more than the intelligence of a six- or seven-year-old. My parents doted on her, kept her safe and protected."

Billy eased into the chair where he had been sitting before as Nick sank back into the sofa. "They died a couple of years ago in a car accident, and since then I've been trying to keep her safe and protected. Unfortunately, no matter how hard I try, I can't seem to teach her that every person in the world isn't a good person."

"People like Sam McClane and Tim O'Brien?" Nick asked.

Billy's eyes hardened and his jaw muscle bunched tightly. "Cheri doesn't know about men, doesn't understand about sex and what an easy target she makes as a pretty woman with the brain of a child. The day I threatened to kill Sam McClane, Cheri and I had gone into town for some shopping. I was paying for groceries and didn't realize she'd wandered off. I found her in the alley with Sam. He had her backed up against the building and was teaching her how to French-kiss. I bloodied his lip and told him the next time he got near her, I'd kill him."

"Same sort of thing happen with Tim O'Brien?" Nick asked. It was difficult to judge a man who'd reacted to a situation exactly the way Nick would have.

Billy nodded. "The circumstances were a little different, but not much. All four of those men didn't know how to keep it in their pants.''

Nick sat up straighter. ''What do you mean? We know Sam McClane was a player...had a wife and a mistress. And apparently everyone in town knew that Tim O'Brien regularly cheated on his wife. But, from everything we've been able to dig up, Greg Maxwell was a devoted, loyal husband and Jonathon Blackbird wasn't even married.''

''Then you aren't digging deep enough when it comes to Maxwell,'' Billy replied. ''Greg and I went to school together. He'd occasionally come out here and share a beer with me.''

''And he told you he was having an affair?''

''Not exactly...I mean, not any real affair. But he told me that he picked up women when he went out of town on business trips. He told me he was unhappy with Virginia and was thinking about divorcing her.''

''Do you know if he told Virginia these things?''

Billy frowned thoughtfully. ''I don't know...I kind of doubt it. Greg was really a nice guy...not into confrontations of any kind. If he had told Virginia he was leaving her, he would have left immediately, and from what I know, they were still together at the time of his death.''

''And Jonathon Blackbird?''

''Jonathon's just a tomcat. He chases after skirts until he gets under one, then moves on to the next.''

Nick tried to assimilate the new information he was gaining. One thing was sure. He didn't believe Billy Thunder had anything to do with the murders of the men. Even without proof of an alibi for the nights in question, Nick couldn't imagine a man caretaking for his mentally challenged sister being responsible for four cold-blooded murders.

"So, you never had any personal run-ins with Greg or Jonathon," he asked, just to be thorough even though he knew the answer already.

"No, like I said, Greg and I were friends. He would have never hurt Cheri. As far as Jonathon was concerned, he never gave me any problems."

"I think we're done here," Nick said and stood. "I appreciate your talking to me. I especially appreciate the fact that you missed me with that shot when we first arrived. Alyssa said that if you'd wanted to, you can have tagged me with no problem."

Billy grinned. "She's right. Sniper training in the army and for the last five years champion shooter in four counties." Billy stood, as well, his expression letting Nick know there was something else on his mind.

"What?" he asked.

Billy hesitated a moment, then spoke. "It's none of my business, but I saw the way you looked at her and the way she looks at you. I don't know what's going on between the two of you, but I have a special affection for Alyssa in my heart. Try not to break hers."

"That would never be my intention," Nick replied. "I'll be waiting for her out in the car."

Nick left the house and walked back to the car. He slid in behind the wheel and waited for Alyssa to join him. Was it obvious to everyone that he wanted Alyssa?

He certainly felt it every minute he spent with her…the desire. It had become an ache inside him that refused to subside, a need that grew bigger each moment until it threatened to consume him.

He desperately wanted to catch the killer that was terrorizing the men in Cherokee Corners, but he was beginning to feel a crazy kind of desperation where Alyssa was concerned, as well.

Alyssa stood with Billy at the front door. "You're running around with a tough crowd these days," he said.

She smiled and looked out the door where she could see Nick waiting in the car. "He's staying at the bed-and-breakfast. You're lucky he didn't instantly arrest you for shooting at him."

"He seems like a stand-up kind of guy."

"I like him." Such simple words for such complicated feelings, she thought.

"I know. I can tell." He smiled at her. "Your eyes never lit up for me the way they do for him. You take care of that heart of yours. I don't want to see it banged up and bruised."

She stretched up on tiptoe and kissed his cheek. "Don't worry about me, Billy. You take care of yourself and Cheri and try to stay out of trouble."

His eyes twinkled merrily. "I try, but trouble seems to find me."

They murmured goodbyes, then Alyssa stepped out

on the porch and walked toward the car. As she walked, she saw Nick's gaze on her. It rivaled the heat of the sun overhead and made her self-consciously aware of the sway of her hips, the thrust of her breasts against her cotton dress and the memory of his lips on hers.

She slid into the passenger seat, wondering if he had any idea how he affected her on such a primal level. Maybe it was because in the untamed visions in her mind, she'd already made love to him a dozen times and now had a lover's awareness of him that was breathtaking.

"Did you get what you needed from Billy?" she asked as she buckled her seat belt.

"Yeah." He put the car in gear and pulled away from Billy's place. "You and Billy...Clay told me you're good friends?" There was a tone in his voice that made her realize he didn't want to know if she and Billy were friends, but he did want to know exactly what kind of relationship she and Billy shared.

"Billy and I have been friends since high school. Both of us were outsiders...me because my fellow students already had begun to identify me as different...weird, and Billy because he was always in trouble."

"In trouble how?"

"Fighting. Somebody was always saying something stupid or unkind about Billy's sister and he was constantly punching somebody out. Anyway, after high school we maintained our friendship, then a couple of years ago we tried to take it one step further. Billy was my first…my only lover.''

She emitted a self-conscious laugh, finding it strange to be discussing this with Nick. ''Our physical relationship only lasted for a few weeks. We knew it wasn't right, that we'd crossed a line that shouldn't have been crossed. I loved Billy, but not in that way. It was a mutual decision that we go back to what we had…a strong friendship but not a romance.''

''Not many people can go backward and continue to maintain a friendship after a physical bond is established and doesn't work out,'' Nick said.

''I wanted to maintain my friendship with Billy, especially after his parents' deaths and him taking over full-time care for Cheri. He's needed a friend over the last couple of years.''

''He's got a tough road to travel,'' Nick agreed. ''His sister is gorgeous.''

''Yes, she is, and has the sunniest disposition you ever want to know. Billy's biggest fear is that some man will take advantage of her.''

''There are men out there who prey on the weak and helpless.'' Nick frowned. ''Have you ever heard any rumors about Greg Maxwell planning on leaving Virginia?''

She looked at him in surprise. ''No, none. Did Billy tell you that?'' He nodded. ''I know Billy and Greg were friends. If it's true, I don't think Virginia knew her husband might be planning on leaving her. Does that information help your investigation?'' she asked.

''I don't know. But Billy pointed out something

that might be the connection between the victims, a connection we haven't been able to come up with.''

''What's that?''

He flashed her a quick glance. ''You don't want to hear about this.''

''Of course I do,'' she replied. ''They are crimes happening in my town, to men I know.'' And you obviously want to talk about it and that makes it all the more important to me. She didn't speak this thought aloud, but it surprised her, the depth of her desire to be the one he shared his thoughts with, even if they were work-related.

''We've all been racking our brains, trying to figure out what the four victims had in common, what the common thread between the four of them were. I think Billy just gave it to us.''

''What's that?''

''All of the men could be considered womanizers. That connection didn't even enter our minds because all we knew was that Greg and Virginia had a happy, committed marriage. But Billy told me that Greg often saw other women when he traveled for business meetings.''

An additional edge of surprise whipped through Alyssa. ''I'd never heard a whisper of Greg being unfaithful to Virginia. If that's the reason he was killed, then somebody had to know about his trysts outside the marriage…somebody besides Billy Thunder.''

''Now all I have to do is figure out who might have

possibly known that fact and if that's what became a motive for murder."

"And if it isn't the motive?"

He flashed her a grin. "Don't try to make my job more difficult than it already is."

She returned his grin. "I wouldn't do that to you."

"On the contrary, you've already made my job more difficult." This time when he gazed at her, a spark of heat radiated from his eyes, a heat that had become familiar to her and washed her with its warmth.

"And how have I done that?" she asked, half-breathless by the sensual ache that shot through her.

"By wearing that flowery perfume that lingers in my head, by having lips that absolutely beg to be kissed, by filling my head with my own set of visions, visions of me making love to you." His voice was low, seductive, even as he laughed. "Alyssa, you have no idea how you've complicated my job."

She was grateful she was sitting down. If she hadn't been, she knew her knees would have buckled beneath her as his words stirred a liquid fire in her veins.

"I feel like I'm being verbally seduced," she murmured.

"Good, because that's what I was trying to do. Unfortunately, unless I remove my hands from the steering wheel, verbal seduction is all I'm capable of at the moment."

"I'd much prefer you keep your hands on the wheel as long as the car is in motion."

That sexy grin curved his lips. ''Of course, I could always pull over.''

''Just drive,'' she said with mock sternness. The sexual energy between them filled the car and pounded inside her. It was a bridled energy that threatened to erupt into something wild and untamed.

Although they continued to talk and banter back and forth for the remainder of the drive home, the tension between them never abated.

Dusk was falling as they got out of his car and entered the bed-and-breakfast through the back door. ''I guess I need to get right into the ice-cream parlor and relieve Mary,'' she said.

He caught her arm as she started to walk away from him. ''She doesn't have to know we're back yet,'' he said as he pulled her into his arms.

Although Alyssa had had every intention of going back to work, the minute he pulled her against him and his lips covered hers in a hot, frantic kiss, she knew she wasn't going into the parlor.

She wasn't going anywhere but up to Nick's room to experience in reality the lovemaking that had merely been, until now, a vision in her mind.

Chapter 9

Nick's kiss left her gasping and weak, and when he finished the kiss and took her by the hand, leading her up the stairs to his room, it didn't enter her mind to protest or play coy. She wanted this...she'd wanted it even before she had met him.

They entered his room, where the dusk light shimmered through the windows, painting the room in golden hues. He closed the door and locked it behind him, then drew her into his arms once again.

She went eagerly, willingly, and felt a rightness in the moment with this man. She felt almost as if this time with Nick had been predecided by the winds of fate and nothing either of them could have done would have stopped this from happening.

His mouth claimed hers hungrily and she responded with a hunger of her own. The kiss was all-consuming…tongue and teeth and breath mingling in erotic prelude.

The kiss seemed to last an eternity. When he finally released her lips, it was merely to taste the hollow of her throat, to nibble the length of her neck. Shivers of pleasure whipped through her as his mouth swept over the sensitive skin.

She wrapped her arms around his neck, molding herself to the hard length of his body as her fingers tangled in the crisp hair at the nape of his neck.

He'd taken away her fear of this moment, had made her recognize how crazy it was to think that anything could make her hurt him. She couldn't begin to understand the end of her vision where Nick was concerned, but she knew nothing in this life could ever make her plunge a knife into another human being, especially Nick. Without the worry, without the fear, she was free to experience their lovemaking without inhibitions.

He framed her face with his hands and looked deep into her eyes. "You take my breath away, Alyssa Whitefeather." His voice was deep, gravelly with want, and she reveled in the sound of it.

She reached up and took hold of his wrists and gently removed his hands from her face, then she stepped back from him. Aware of his hot gaze watching her every movement, she walked over to the bed and pulled off the blue gingham comforter. It fell to the floor, exposing the pastel blue sheets beneath.

"Now, that's what I call turndown service," he said gruffly. He pulled his cell phone from his pocket and set it on the dresser, unfastened his ankle holster and placed it and his gun next to the phone. Then he joined her at the side of the bed.

"When I first saw you wearing pink, I thought that was a great color on you." His voice was low, sweetly seductive as his fingers worked to unfasten the top button of her sundress. "Then on the day of Clay's wedding I saw you in that green and I thought that was definitely your color."

His fingers moved to the second button and Alyssa's breath caught at his slow, methodical movements. In her vision they had already been in bed, had already been in the act itself.

The vision had revealed nothing of their foreplay, had given her no indication of how mesmerizing his gaze would be, how achingly magnificent his simplest touch would be. Her vision hadn't prepared her for his sensual assault on all her senses.

As he undid each button, his fingertips brushed each inch of newly exposed skin. Her heart raced with a rhythm it had never felt before...a pounding she seemed to feel in every nerve in her body.

"I love the way you look in red," he murmured as he unfastened the button at her waist. "But I think I'm going to like you best of all dressed in those blue sheets and me."

New shivers of anticipation fluttered through her as he slid the dress off her shoulders and it tumbled to the floor around her feet.

She wasn't sure if it was the cool air in the room

or the flames in Nick's eyes that made her nipples harden against the thin silk of her bra.

She reached up for his shirt buttons, her fingers slightly clumsy as she worked on unfastening the first one. "And I'd love to be wearing just those blue sheets...and you." She leaned forward and pressed her lips against the bare skin of his hard-muscled chest. She heard the hiss as he drew a quick breath, and her fingers worked faster to undo the last of the buttons.

When she was finished, he whipped the shirt off as if the fabric burned his skin. Then he quickly unfastened his slacks and stepped out of them.

Alyssa had never known that simple men's white briefs could be so sexy, but on Nick's lean-muscled, highly aroused body, they were far more than sexy. She scarcely had time to admire him before he tumbled them both onto the bed.

She was on her back as his mouth sought hers again. He leaned over her, his body warm...almost fevered against her own.

When he lifted his mouth from hers, he smiled. "Just as I suspected. You look more beautiful now than ever."

The heat in his eyes simmered inside her. "When you look at me like that you make me feel more beautiful than I've ever felt in my life."

He kissed her again as one of his hands reached beneath her to unclasp her bra. When he'd accomplished his goal he pushed the bra up and covered one of her bare breasts with his hand.

A soft moan escaped her at the intimate contact. His mouth left hers and blazed a trail down her throat, down to capture one of her nipples between his lips.

She pulled her bra off and tossed it aside, wanting nothing to interfere with his pleasure…with her own pleasure.

As his tongue lathed first one nipple then the other, she ran her hand across the broad expanse of his back, loving the way his muscled yet supple skin felt beneath her fingertips.

She twined her legs with his and pressed her hips against his hardness. Even with the material of her panties and his briefs between them, she could feel him throbbing against her.

She reached down, wanting to touch him, but he stopped her by grabbing her hand. He raised his head and looked at her. With the twilight shadows beginning to fill the room, his eyes appeared almost silver.

"Alyssa, it's been three years since I've been with any woman. I'm afraid if you touch me it will be over before either of us wants it to be."

"But I want to give you pleasure," she protested breathlessly.

"Oh, darlin', you are, but at the moment I want to pleasure you before I take you completely." He lowered his head to her breasts once again, and at the same time one of his hands smoothed down her stomach. His touch lingered for a moment at the band of her panties, caressing the skin just above the silk barrier.

Alyssa's entire body trembled with the onslaught

of new sensations. She caught her breath as he touched her there…at her center, stroking her through the silk of her panties.

She moaned again, this time louder as nerve endings responded to his intimate touch. It was impossible to remain still and just accept. Her hips moved without volition, in rhythm with his stroking fingers, as an unbearable tension rose inside her.

As the pressure built, she was carried to a place in her mind where thought, either rational or irrational, was impossible. There was no room inside her for thoughts or visions or anything else but Nick.

As he stroked her fast, the pressure inside her exploded. She cried out his name as ripples then thunderous waves of pleasure crashed through her.

Nick's hands shook as he slid the panties down her slender hips and to her knees. As she kicked them off, he fought to maintain his control. His desire to possess her was like a raging wild beast inside him. It clawed at his insides with a need he'd never believed he'd feel again.

She looked so beautiful against the pale sheets, with her hair a spill of darkness, and her soft, dusky skin and her mysterious eyes appearing bluer than he'd ever seen them.

From the moment he'd tumbled her onto the bed, his desire had raged almost beyond his control. He'd had to concentrate on maintaining his own control while coaxing her to lose all of her control. It had been like walking a tightrope.

Pleasuring her had electrified him, and he knew if he didn't make love to her at this moment it would be too late.

He kicked off the briefs that had become not only irritating but constrictive, as well, then moved on top of her. She opened her legs to him, her eyes half-closed with obvious sensual joy. As he entered her wet tightness, a deep groan escaped him.

Buried inside her, he remained completely still for a long moment, afraid that any movement at all would send him over the edge, and he wasn't ready...not yet, for their lovemaking to be over so quickly.

Her fingertips nipped into his back, not sharp enough to be painful, but hard enough to be erotic.

"Nick," she said softly, and he covered her hot, sweet mouth with his as he moved his hips back to begin the dance of lovemaking.

He could feel her heartbeat crashing against his own as he began to thrust into her. She met him thrust for thrust, and the intensity of sensation made his senses reel.

Faster they moved as twilight deepened and shadows moved to usurp the last of day's light. Nick was lost...lost in the splendor of her.

It wasn't until she cried out and stiffened beneath him that he realized he'd brought her to climax once again and it was then that he reached his own.

It was as he spilled into her that he realized he hadn't thought about birth control. He wasn't concerned about disease issues, neither of them could be classified as promiscuous by any measure. But he also wasn't prepared to become a daddy.

He had grown to care about Alyssa, and certainly she had reawakened a part of him that had been dead for a very long time, but he was realistic enough to know that his time with her was not permanent. She had her work, her life here, and his was back in Tulsa.

He remained unmoving for a long moment, allowing his heartbeat and breathing to return to a more normal rhythm. He raised onto one elbow and gazed down at her. It was amazing that even though he was spent and utterly sated, just looking at her renewed a touch of hunger inside him.

With two fingers he brushed an errant strand of hair away from her eyes. "I'm not usually irresponsible," he began.

"I've been on birth control pills for the past year because of irregular periods. I'm assuming you were telling me the truth about not being with anyone for three years."

He smiled. "And I'm assuming you were telling me the truth when you said you've only had one lover before me."

"Now that we have that out of the way, I should get up and go relieve Mary."

He tightened his arms around her. "Not yet. Don't you realize that the moments spent in the afterglow of lovemaking are just as important as the lovemaking itself?"

"I can't believe that sentiment is coming from a man," she said teasingly. Her eyes sparkled and he was pleased that he'd been the man to put the sparkle there. "I thought men were always the first ones to jump out of bed or fall asleep to avoid any kind of emotional intimacy."

"That's a myth. Men enjoy pillow talk as much as women do," he protested. It was impossible to remain next to her and not touch her in some way. He ran a finger down her cheek, loving the feel of her soft skin.

"I've never done pillow talk before... What do people talk about?" she asked curiously.

Despite the fact that she was almost thirty years old and suffered from some sort of psychic visions of death and horror, Nick was struck by what an innocent she truly was. A surprising protectiveness welled up inside him for her.

"They talk about lots of things...like how their day went, what they want for dinner, what they want in the future."

She laughed, a low, throaty laugh that made him recognize he'd want her again...soon. "So, what do you want for dinner?" she asked. "If you had to choose your most favorite dinner, what would it be?"

"That's easy. Thanksgiving Day dinner, although I'm not sure if it was the food or the family that always made that meal special." He rolled over on his back and folded his arms beneath his head. "Turkey and corn-bread stuffing, mashed potatoes and giblet gravy...and laughter and old stories and new friends."

"You have a big family?" She propped herself up on one elbow, her dainty hand resting on his chest.

''Not really. It's just my parents and my sister, Judy. They all live in Chicago. Judy is a schoolteacher, divorced and without children. Things were different when Dorrie was alive. She'd plan the holiday dinner and invite family and dozens of friends and co-workers.''

He smiled, hoping he hadn't offended her by bringing up Dorrie's name. ''What about you? Whatever made you decide to open a bed-and-breakfast?''

There was just enough light left in the room for him to see her lovely features. She frowned and gently tangled her hand in his tuft of chest hair. ''I don't know, I guess because I decided early on that I didn't really want to go to college. I loved to bake and didn't mind cleaning and it seemed like a good way for me to make a living and be independent.''

She untangled her hand from his chest hair and instead smoothed it over the expanse of his chest, her expression still thoughtful. ''My aunt and uncle had invested my parents' life insurance money for me, so I used that to buy this place and get it into shape.''

''Are you happy doing this?''

His question seemed to jar her. Her hand stopped its movement and her pretty, blue eyes appeared troubled. ''I don't know...I guess. I usually don't have time to know if I'm happy or not.''

''You must meet all kinds of people.'' He was trying to keep focused on their conversation, but was finding it increasingly difficult. Her body was so warm against his and her hair fell just over his shoulder like a sensuous sweep of silk.

"I've had all kinds of people stay here," she agreed. "Nice people and some not-so-great people. The good thing is, most of them don't stay long… usually a couple of days and then they're gone." She frowned again. "Of course, Tamara, Clay's wife, tells me that's why I went into this kind of business in the first place, so I wouldn't have to deal with anything but superficial relationships."

"Is that true?" Despite being distracted by her physical nearness, this part of the conversation piqued his interest once again.

"I don't know…maybe." Her hand stopped moving altogether and instead reached up to grab a strand of her hair. She twisted it around her fingers as she continued. "I've always kept a certain amount of distance between myself and others."

"Because of your visions?"

She nodded. "Nobody seems to understand the full effect the visions have on me and how afraid I am to open myself up completely to anyone."

"I can't pretend to know what it's like to suffer from visions," Nick said. "But if you never open yourself up to anyone, then you'll never know the full pleasure of friendship or true, mature love. All your relationships will be like the ones you have with your guests…brief and superficial."

She didn't reply. She lay her head back on the pillow and released a small sigh. For a moment they remained like that, side by side and silent.

He wondered what she was thinking, surprised to discover that he cared what thoughts worried her. He sensed her restlessness before she made a move. A moment later she sighed once again and sat up.

"I've got to get dressed and go downstairs," she said.

"Why? Mary doesn't know how to close up the ice-cream parlor?" He realized what he really wanted at this moment was to fall asleep with her in his bed, in his arms. He had a feeling that's what she needed more than anything else in the world at the moment…for somebody to hold her through the dark and lonely night.

"Of course she knows how to close up," she replied.

"Then stay." He took her arm and pulled her back down next to him.

"But there are things I need to do," she protested, even as she snuggled up next to him.

"What things do you need to do that can't wait until morning?" he asked, smoothing her hair as she nuzzled her face into the crook of his neck.

A sense of tranquillity stole through him as he realized she wasn't going anywhere. Along with the tranquillity came a bone-deep weariness as the last couple of days of early mornings and late nights caught up with him.

Apparently she suffered an exhaustion deeper than a mere day's work, for within minutes he knew that she'd fallen sound asleep. She slept like a baby, soundlessly, curled up against him to create a warm cocoon at his side.

For Nick, sleep was more elusive. He watched as

night completely claimed the room, plunging everything into darkness except for the faint illumination from his clock and cell phone on the dresser.

Making love to Alyssa had been the first thing Nick had done in a long time that had felt absolutely right. However, he was smart enough to realize that the basis of her attraction to him was a vision that had visited her before she'd ever even met him.

He knew their circumstances weren't exactly normal, and he couldn't be sure how real any feelings they thought they might have for each other were. He wasn't even sure of his own feelings where she was concerned.

He wanted her. Physically she drew him to her with a heady desire that was impossible to ignore. She intrigued him, as well...the visions, the sadness he sometimes saw radiating from her eyes, the hunger for something more that he sensed inside her.

But that didn't mean that anything that happened now between them would last after the serial killer had been caught and her visions about him had stopped. Thankfully, he didn't have to sort any of it out tonight, he thought as he felt sleep finally edging closer.

He knew he was dreaming...knew because everything was black and white. Since Dorrie's murder, his dreams had lost all their color. In the dream, he wandered the center square. The streets were deserted, the stores all closed up for the night. Not a living soul broke the silence of the night that surrounded him, but the dead were there.

Greg Maxwell leaned against the public-library doors and waved at him as he walked by. Sam McClane raised a hand from his spot in front of the post office. Tim O'Brien grinned and tipped an imaginary hat from the bench in front of the hardware store and Jonathon Blackbird sat on a tree limb above the place where his body had been found.

Then he was no longer walking the square, but was in a copse of trees with Alyssa, and colors exploded around him...the sharp blue of her eyes, the brilliant green of the leaves on the trees, the bright yellow of the blanket beneath them.

The sharpness of the colors after the visions in black and white nearly blinded him and he held on to her, lost not only in the visual magnificence, but also in the splendor of making love to her.

They rolled over so she was on top, controlling their sexual rhythm. Her eyes, which had shone with pleasure moments before, deepened in hue, becoming dark...darker, then black. A mocking, derisive smile curved her lips, then her arms were over her head and in her hands was a knife.

Pain, sharper than any he'd ever experienced in his life, ripped through him as she slammed the knife into his chest. Blood, so red it hurt to look at, spurted from the wound. With a laugh of glee, she stabbed him again...and again...and her eyes glistened with the joy of the kill.

He sat straight up, his heart racing with terror, his

brain working to orient himself. He gasped and glanced at the bedside clock. Almost 2:00 a.m. His cell phone rang and he realized the jarring sound was what had pulled him from the horrific nightmare.

Trying not to awaken Alyssa, he crept from the bed and grabbed the phone from the dresser. As he answered, the night-light was turned on and Alyssa sat up, her gaze intent on him.

He listened to the voice at the other end of the line, then replied curtly, "I'll be right there."

"What?" Alyssa asked as he hung up. "What's happened, Nick?"

"We don't have to worry about Michael Stanmeyer being our serial killer," he said as he reached for his clothes.

"Why not?" Her eyes were huge as she clutched the sheet to her naked breast.

"That was one of the cops on night patrol. They just found Michael in the center square. He's been stabbed."

He heard the swift intake of Alyssa's breath. "Is he…is he dead?"

"He was alive when they found him." Nick strapped on his ankle holster, then stepped into a pair of slacks. He had a bad feeling…a very bad feeling.

He wasn't sure if it was because of the disturbing dream he'd just suffered or because of the news he'd just received. But as his gaze met Alyssa's, he suddenly realized a connection he hadn't made before.

Men in Cherokee Corners were being stabbed to death, and for the past month Alyssa had been having visions of herself stabbing a man to death. Was there a connection? Was she tapped into some sort of energy she didn't even realize or understand?

There was no time to question the issue with her now, but he realized no matter how painful it was for her, no matter how uncomfortable the visions made her and despite his desire to protect her, they were going to have to explore the depths of her psychic abilities.

He was beginning to think that perhaps Alyssa's mind might hold the only key that would lead to their killer.

Chapter 10

"I can't believe it. I just can't believe that weird Michael is dead." Virginia reached across the table and helped herself to another blueberry muffin.

"I'd rather you not call him that," Alyssa said without the patience she usually used with the often thoughtless, attractive widow. "Especially now. You should have a little respect for the dead."

The two women were alone in the dining room. Alyssa's irritation with Virginia had begun earlier that morning when Virginia had first come down for breakfast and Alyssa had hurried upstairs to make her bed and clean the room.

At that time, neither of them had heard the news about Michael. Alyssa's first irritation with Virginia had come when she'd seen that the woman had apparently spilled fingernail polish remover all over the nightstand, ruining the finish on the cherrywood.

Virginia had been a less-than-perfect boarder during her stay, but Alyssa had been reluctant to ask her to leave, knowing how Virginia dreaded going back to the lovely home she'd shared with her murdered husband.

She'd finished cleaning the room, then had hurried back downstairs when the phone had rung. Virginia took the call, and when she'd hung up, she'd announced to Alyssa that Michael had been attacked the night before and had died before they'd gotten him to the hospital.

"You're right, that wasn't nice of me," Virginia agreed easily. "But, honestly, Alyssa, you have to admit that he was strange."

"He was painfully shy," Alyssa replied, a lump in her throat as she thought of Michael. "I noticed when I was cleaning earlier that you've spilled something on the nightstand in your room…" She hadn't really meant to say anything, but the woman's irreverence toward Michael pushed her buttons.

"Fingernail polish remover. I'm so sorry." She pursed her pouty lips in a gesture of apology. "I'll pay for a new nightstand." She set her muffin on the plate in front of her and her eyes suddenly teared up. "Greg used to say that nail polish was as sexy as black hose. He loved it when I painted my nails."

She stared down at her hands, the nails at the moment unpolished but neatly manicured. "I keep trying to polish them. I'll put polish on one hand, but then I start thinking about Greg and…and…I just can't do it."

A little choking sob escaped her and Alyssa felt like a total jerk for even mentioning the blemished surface. "Don't worry about the nightstand," she said. "I'm sure I've got a replacement someplace in storage."

Virginia dabbed at her tears with her napkin, then picked up the blueberry muffin once again. "I thought you were expecting new guests to check in."

Alyssa blinked to rapidly process Virginia's quick-silver change of topic and mood. "Yes, they were booked to stay for the next three nights, but they called and canceled due to illness."

It was probably a good thing the couple from Des Moines had canceled their stay. Alyssa knew it wouldn't be long and the police would be at the bed-and-breakfast, inside Michael's bedroom, searching for clues to who might have wanted him dead.

She left Virginia at the table and returned to the kitchen, her thoughts still focused on the tall, thin, quiet man who had been her boarder for almost two years.

Last night they'd entertained the thought that he might be the serial killer. Today he was a tragic victim. She didn't even know if he had family, if there was somebody who needed to be contacted, if somebody would even miss his very presence on earth.

She hadn't known Michael well, hadn't taken the time to get to know him. But her heart broke as she thought of him stabbed and left naked someplace in the area. Poor Michael.

She poured herself a cup of coffee and sat at the

kitchen island, her thoughts leaving Michael and turning to Nick and the night they had spent together.

It wasn't exactly morning-after regrets that weighed on her mind, but it was a wary acknowledgment that as wonderful as last night had been, it had simply been one night and nothing more.

Nick was getting too close, invading areas inside her she'd never opened to anyone else and that frightened her a little. Her natural instinct, the instinct that had served her well for her entire life, was to pull back and protect herself.

Nick would hopefully solve the murders, then would leave Cherokee Corners. She would remain here, living her life with her visions as company and entertaining superficial relationships with the guests who came and went.

Her grandmother had told her long ago that she would probably live her life alone, that people with the special gift of visions were usually alone, and it was best if she reconciled herself to that fact early in her life.

When her grandmother had died and she'd gone to live with the James family, even though love and support had surrounded her, she'd felt the aloneness her grandmother had spoken of. She hadn't quite fit in anywhere for the entirety of her life. Her visions had deemed her odd, separate, and that's the way she'd felt for most of her life.

The only time she hadn't felt that feeling was last night, when she'd been in Nick's arms. But, with the light of day shining full through the kitchen windows, she knew better than to pretend that she and Nick would be anything more than a brief relationship while he was in town.

Nick was her gift to herself, a treasure that she could remember long after he was gone. Besides, she was probably just a transition kind of woman for Nick, the first one to reawaken him after Dorrie's death. Perhaps that was all she was meant to be in his life.

She had learned at her grandmother's knee not to question or fight fate, but rather to accept what life brought in the Cherokee way…with dignity and strength.

"Alyssa?" Virginia poked her head into the kitchen. "I'm going upstairs now to lie down. All this commotion has made me feel sick and I have a headache coming on. I just thought I'd let you know so you could go ahead and clear off the breakfast things."

Alyssa nodded and waved a hand at the pretty blonde. She wasn't the only one with a headache. Alyssa had been fighting one since awakening to the news that Michael had been stabbed. She finished drinking her coffee, then wearily pulled herself up and out of her chair.

She hadn't gone back to sleep after the phone call that had taken Nick away in the middle of the night. Even though she had left his room and gone downstairs to her own bed, sleep had refused to revisit her.

It was just before eleven o'clock when they arrived. Alyssa had finished cleaning up the dining room and kitchen, when Nick and two men she'd never seen before walked in the front door.

Nick quickly introduced her to the others, Bud and Tony, and told her they were his partners from Tulsa. "We need you to open up Michael's room for us," he said.

She nodded solemnly, although there were a million questions she wanted to ask him. Had Michael told them anything before he'd died? Were they able to get any clues at all as to who was terrorizing the men in town?

Although she wanted to ask, she knew this wasn't the place or the time. The grim lines that bracketed his mouth and the dark shadows in his eyes let her know that Nick was fully immersed in the job they had to do.

She pulled her master keys from her dress pocket and escorted the men to Michael's door. Although she'd wanted to enter the room immediately when she'd heard that her boarder had died, she'd realized to do so might compromise the investigation.

If she had been expecting to see strange and bewildering things in the room, she would have been disappointed. The room was as neat and clean as when she'd first shown it to Michael.

She watched from the doorway as Nick and his two partners began to look around the room. Bud went to the closet, where he searched the pockets of the meager number of clothes hanging inside. Tony looked under the bed and then disappeared into the bathroom while Nick walked over to the table, where a laptop computer was closed and a neat stack of blank paper set next to it.

"Stanmeyer ever mention any family at all?" He opened the laptop and booted it up.

"No, none," she replied.

"What about mail? Did he ever receive any mail?"

"Not here, but it's possible he had a post-office box rented."

"Nothing here," Tony said from the bathroom.

"Check the drawers. Someplace this man has to have somebody who might give a damn that he's dead."

Nick's voice was coldly determined and all business and Alyssa realized she was seeing a side of him she'd never seen before. Instead of the teasing, sexy, friendly man she'd come to know, he was now a professional profiler, looking for clues, seeking the road map that would take him into the mind of a killer.

"From what we've learned so far, it would appear our Mr. Stanmeyer was an English professor from California," Nick said as his fingers worked the mouse on the laptop.

"An English professor?" Alyssa took a step into the room. "I wonder what brought him here."

"Apparently three years ago he applied for disability from social security because of severe panic attacks that made it impossible for him to teach. He was granted disability and told his co-workers that he was moving to a small town and was going to try to write a book."

A wave of sadness swept through Alyssa as she

thought of Michael. Nick seemed to sense her feelings. "It wasn't like the others," he said softly. "He'd been stabbed, but he was found fully dressed."

Alyssa wasn't sure, but somehow that made it easier, that the killer hadn't stripped him naked and left him for his fellow townspeople to see. "But was it the same killer?"

"We don't know yet. We're waiting for the medical examiner to tell us."

"I'll just leave you all to do your work," she said and started to back out of the room. "Just let me know when you're finished and I'll lock the room once again."

She went back down to the kitchen, drained of what little energy she'd awakened possessing. It didn't take long for the phone to begin ringing. She received calls from her aunt Rita, her "sisters," Breanna and Savannah, and her new sister-in-law and best friend, Tamara. She also got calls from the curious, looking for more information about the latest murder.

Nick and his team remained upstairs for about an hour and a half, then they left, but not before Nick told her she was temporarily shut down. "Don't let anyone in or out of here except Virginia," he said. "No new guests for the time being."

She nodded and he paused before turning to leave. "You okay?" he asked softly.

"Yes…just sad."

"Yeah, well, I'm past being sad and I'm moving quickly into the pissed-off stage." With these words he turned and left.

The silence of the house reverberated around her and she returned to the kitchen island and sat, trying to decide if she wanted to make another pot of coffee or not. She opted against it. She'd already had too much caffeine and it was just after noon.

A knock on the front door carried her back to the living room and the front entrance of the bed-and-breakfast.

She opened the door to see Scott Moberly standing there, his freckled face lit with eager anticipation. She considered slamming the door as quickly as possible rather than having to talk to the overeager young newspaper reporter. But she'd learned when her aunt Rita had been missing that Scott was nothing if not tenacious.

"Hey, Alyssa." He smiled brightly as she stepped out onto the porch.

"What do you want, Scott?" Alyssa had mixed feelings about Scott. He was one of the few people in town who knew with absolute certainty that Alyssa sometimes had visions.

He'd covered a case of a missing child several years ago and one of Alyssa's visions had led the police to the child, who'd gotten lost and had curled up in an old shed and had fallen asleep.

Scott had overheard a heated discussion between Alyssa and the lead officer assigned to the case. The lead officer had written her off as a nut and refused to pay any attention to what she was telling him about the child's whereabouts.

It had taken a lot of pleading and begging from

Alyssa to make Scott promise to keep her out of his newspaper article on the case. Thankfully, Scott's need to please people often got into the way of his reporting. Reluctantly he'd agreed not to use her name.

"What do I want? Jeez, Alyssa, what do you think I want? I know you've got the FBI guy staying here, one of the victim's wives here, and now one of your boarders has been murdered." He held a pencil and pad at the ready. "So, what are your thoughts about all this?"

"No comment," she replied.

Scott frowned in dismay. "Ah, come on, Alyssa, don't be like that. Have you *seen* anything…you know what I mean?"

"No, Scott." She sighed wearily. "There's no story here, nothing I can give you that would make interesting, newsworthy reading."

Scott's smile fell. "Anything interesting you can tell me about Michael Stanmeyer? Nobody around here seems to have known much about him."

She shook her head. "No. Honestly, Scott, if I knew anything at all, I'd tell you. But you probably know more about these murders than I do."

"Probably not much more," Scott said, obviously disheartened. "Since the FBI moved in I can't get anyone to tell me anything. Even the local cops have clammed up."

"I'm sorry, Scott. There's nothing I can tell you."

"Okay…well, thanks anyway, Alyssa."

She watched as Scott left the porch and headed in

the direction of Ruby's. He was probably hoping to find a story in the gossip of the late-lunch group.

Her gaze went to the park setting across the street. She'd always loved the fact that the city had long ago proclaimed that the center of the square would remain a park area, with no buildings to mar the natural beauty of the wooded area.

Now the park seemed to seethe with secrets, with shadowed darkness where a murderer could meet an intended victim, where evil made plans and carried them out.

For a long moment she scanned the tree line, looking for a tree that resembled the one that had haunted her, but none of the full-foliaged trees looked like the misshapen one in her vision.

She went back inside to her private quarters. She sank down on the sofa and drew a deep breath, fighting the headache that had been pounding at her temples since she'd awakened that morning.

In the last hour the headache had intensified along with a sense of imminent doom. She knew the feeling far too well. It was a vision trying to appear. It was a vision seeking to make itself known.

She also recognized she didn't have the strength to fight against it. She was too tired, and the morning had already held too many emotional upsets for her to be strong enough to reject the darkness that had begun to obscure her sight.

With a sigh of resignation she allowed the vision to take her through the familiar tunnel of darkness and to the other side where her mind filled with the same vision that had come to her for over a month.

Their lovemaking brought tears of pleasure to her eyes. The caress of Nick's hands, the heat of his kiss, all brought her an exquisite pleasure that she knew she'd want to experience over and over again.

The tears of joy vanished as the scene changed. She was on top of Nick beneath the gnarled tree and the knife handle was cool and familiar in her fingers.

As she plunged the knife into his chest, his blood ran hot as his blue eyes filled with a horror that shot a surge of power through her.

She came to gasping, sprawled on her sofa with her heart beating frantically and a residual taste of wicked domination in her mouth.

She sat up and drew several deep, cleansing breaths in an effort to further remove herself from the nightmare her mind had just presented to her.

Her legs were shaky as she stood, a growing sense of horror sweeping through her. She'd believed that in actually making love with Nick, this particular vision would halt.

That's the way it had always been in the past. When the vision was resolved with reality, the vision passed and she had it no more.

When her aunt Rita had been kidnapped and held, she'd had visions of her until she'd been found, then that particular vision had come to her no more.

She'd *seen* herself making love to a man she didn't know, a man who had arrived in town and whom she'd now made love with. So, why was she still having the vision?

She knew she would never, *could* never stab Nick, yet that's what her vision showed her over and over again.

It was going to happen. Horror swept through her. It wouldn't be her, but at some time somebody was going to stab Nick. She knew it with a certainty that filled her with icy terror. Sooner or later, Nick was going to be stabbed to death.

Chapter 11

It was after eight when Nick made his way back to the bed-and-breakfast. He was surprised to see the ice-cream parlor windows dark, the Closed sign turned outward.

When he'd told Alyssa to shut down the bed-and-breakfast, he hadn't meant for her to close the parlor, as well. He pulled around to the back parking lot and pulled into an empty space. He cut the engine, but didn't move to get out of the car right away.

He worried his hand through his hair, then released a deep sigh. This case was making him crazy. He'd only worked one case before where getting into the killer's mind had been so difficult, where getting into his skin seemed so impossible, and that had been Murphy.

Nick hadn't felt this defeated since the days immediately following Dorrie's murder when his rage had left him empty and bereft.

They had no viable suspects. It was as simple as that. Initially, Virginia had been a suspect when her husband had been murdered. As was always the case, the first suspect in a murder was a spouse or family member. But the death of Sam McClane had prompted the police to look elsewhere for their killer. Dammit, he'd never worked a case that had so little to go on, so lacking in suspects.

He'd thought about stopping by Ruby's to get something to eat, since lunch had been a slice of pizza on the run, and dinner had been skipped altogether. But ultimately he hadn't wanted to go into the busy diner and face the curious glances or questions about the most recent murder from fellow patrons.

Wearily he pulled himself out of the car and dragged himself to the back door. Alyssa was waiting for him just inside and despite his weariness his heart leaped a bit at the sight of her.

Her hair was loose around her shoulders and she was clad in a simple off-white sundress that emphasized the beautiful bronze tones of her skin and the shapely curves she possessed. It was only when he looked into her eyes that his pleasure was swept away by concern.

"What's wrong?"

Her eyes were the blue-gray of an overcast sky. "We need to talk," she said as she took him by the arm and led him to her private quarters.

Something in her dark eyes disturbed him. "Has something happened?" he asked.

She shook her head and didn't speak again until they were in the privacy of her small living room. She sat on the sofa and pulled him down next to her. She released his hand but held his gaze intently. "I'm afraid for you, Nick." Emotion filled her soft-spoken words. "I'm so terribly afraid for you."

He took her hands in his...they were cold, like twin ice cubes. "What's going on, Alyssa? What are you afraid of?"

She tightened her grip on his hands, her fingers taking the warmth from his. "I thought once we made love...once we acted on the vision, then it would go away. That's the way it's always happened in the past... The vision is resolved with reality, then I never have it again."

"But you're still having the same one?" he guessed.

She nodded, the movement jerky and oddly un-coordinated-looking. She pulled her hands from his and jumped up off the sofa and began to pace before him with short, quick steps.

"I had it again this morning...the exact same vision."

"I'd hate to think that the only reason you made love with me was to banish a disturbing vision," he said in an attempt to lighten the mood.

She stopped in her tracks and stared at him wide-eyed. "Of course that's not the reason I slept with you." Her cheeks colored slightly. "I slept with you because I wanted to…I desperately wanted to make love with you.'' She reached a hand up, as if to grasp the ends of her hair, but instead dropped the hand back to her side and began to pace once again. ''It's not done…that's what scares me.''

''What's not done?''

''The vision! It's not done.'' She sighed in obvious frustration. ''Before I met you, and even immediately after you came here, I was afraid that somehow I would be responsible for stabbing you to death.''

''But you know that isn't going to happen.'' He frowned, unable to figure out exactly what had her so obviously disturbed. ''Alyssa, would you stop pacing and sit down here and tell me what's going on in that pretty head of yours?''

''Your murder, that's what's going on in my head.'' She didn't so much as sit as throw herself back on the sofa next to him.

This time it was her hands that reached for his and she held on to him, squeezing his fingers tightly. ''I thought you'd be safe because I knew I'd never stab you, no matter what the circumstances. But I realized today that it's possible the hands I see in the vision, the hands that wield the knife and stab you, might not be my own.''

''Is it possible you're seeing the killer's hands?'' Nick felt a renewed burst of energy course through him.

He'd wondered before about Alyssa's vision…if the answer to the killer's identity might somehow be inside her mind, but dealing with Michael's murder had driven the thought out of his mind. Now he was riveted by the idea that her vision might contain something…anything that would lead them to the murderer.

"There's something about the vision I haven't told you." She broke eye contact with him and instead looked down at the carpeting at their feet. Once again a deep frown cut into her forehead, worrying him as he waited as patiently as possible for her to continue.

Her hands were warmer now, as if by speaking to him some of the fear that had turned them ice cold had dissipated. "In the vision…when I'm stabbing you…I feel something…something awful."

"What do you mean, awful?"

"A huge rush of power sweeps through me. I feel powerful and strong, almost giddy with self-righteous glee." She flashed him a dark glance, then looked down again. "But the worst part is that while a part of me thinks it's awful, there's another part of me that loves that rush of utter domination."

Adrenaline spiked through Nick at her words. "Have you ever tried to consciously summon your visions?"

She gazed at him in surprise. "No. Usually I'm too busy trying to be strong enough to shove them away."

"Do you think you could summon your vision at will?"

"I…I don't know. I've never tried before. Why?"

"I think somehow you're tapped into the killer's mind. I think that maybe somewhere in your vision is the clue we need to break this case.'' He'd expected his words to shock her, but she merely nodded, as if she'd already reached this same conclusion.

"So, what do you want me to do?''

He released her hands but held her gaze. "I want you to try to bring on the vision and I want to see if somehow I can get into the vision with you.''

"What do you mean?'' she asked curiously. "How can you get in it with me?''

"I'm hoping that if you go into a vision, somehow I can talk to you while you're there—'' He broke off in frustration. "I don't know if you'll be able to hear me or not. I don't know if you'll be able to answer questions or not. But I think we need to try it, don't you?''

A touch of fear darkened her eyes and he put his arm around her shoulders and drew her close to his side. She leaned into him, feeling small and vulnerable, and a sense of protectiveness battled with his sense of duty. "I know it's a terrible thing to see, a terrible thing to feel. But I'll be right here to see that everything is all right.''

"I want to help…but I'm afraid.''

"I won't let anything happen to you,'' he said, although he knew it might be an empty promise despite his best intentions.

He didn't know what possible consequences she might pay for delving deep into her dark vision and potentially sharing the mind of a killer.

"On second thought, maybe this isn't such a good idea. You don't have to do this.''

"But I do," she replied. "I don't want to consciously try to summon up that terrible scene, the horrible feelings the vision brings to me, but I have to. If there is even a tiny chance that somehow my vision holds the key to the killer's identity, I have to try to find it."

"Are you sure?"

She nodded, and as she reached up to grab the ends of her hair, her fingers trembled slightly. "We have to try this, Nick. If for no other reason than to save your life."

Her words haunted him. Although he couldn't imagine a situation where he would be at the mercy of anyone with a knife, the frightened certainty in her eyes sent a chill up his spine.

"You want to lie down or something?" he asked and stood from the sofa.

She smiled then shook her head ruefully. "I've never tried to do this before, so I don't know if I need to lie down or not. My visions come to me when I'm standing, sitting or in bed. It doesn't seem to matter what physical position I'm in. It's a matter of allowing my mind to be open enough, unguarded enough to allow in a vision."

"I'd feel better about this if you were lying down," he said. "I can't help but remember that the last time you had a vision when I was around, you passed out and would have hit the deck if I hadn't caught you."

"You're right," she agreed. "I probably should be lying down."

She stretched out on the sofa and Nick pulled a

chair up next to her. He wasn't sure who was more nervous, her or him. They were attempting to do something she'd never done before...call on a vision and attempt to interact with it. He'd certainly never tried anything this unorthodox before.

She closed her eyes and drew several deep breaths, each time letting the air out slowly. "I just need to empty my mind, let my natural defenses shut down," she murmured more to herself than to him.

He sat close enough to her that he could smell the scent of her, the slightly sweet, freshly clean scent he'd come to identify with her. His gaze swept over her features, lingering on the long length of her dark eyelashes, her high cheekbones, her straight nose and the full lips that even now seemed to beg him for a kiss.

Warmth centered in his stomach and spread out rivers of heat through his veins. It wasn't the heat of desire, but rather a softer, sweeter heat. The warmth of caring and protectiveness, and something precariously close to love.

Her eyes sprang open and she smiled apologetically. "This might take a while. I'm so accustomed to keeping my mind busy, guarding against the darkness that always brings the vision."

"There's no hurry. Take your time, and if it doesn't work, it doesn't work." He returned her smile, wanting her to know that it was all right if this crazy idea wasn't successful.

Once again she closed her eyes and he fought back the instinct to tell her to forget it, that there had to be another way besides her going back to the scene that caused her such anguish.

Seconds ticked by…minutes in which Nick's heart beat with the frantic rhythm of stress and anticipation. She was silent and so still he suspected she might have fallen asleep, but her breathing told him otherwise. She breathed too fast, too uneven to be asleep.

He expected her to open her eyes at any moment and tell him it was useless to try, that there was no way she could consciously summon the vision they sought.

He watched her features expectantly, looking for any signs of distress or discomfort, ready to pull the plug on the whole experiment if he thought she was in some sort of psychological danger.

The first sign he got that something was going on inside her head was that beneath her eyelids he saw her eyes frantically moving. He leaned forward, careful not to touch her. If she had succeeded in summoning the vision, he didn't want to pull her out of it, but he did want to be a part of it.

''Alyssa,'' he said softly. She didn't reply, but her eyes continued to move rapidly beneath her eyelids. ''Alyssa, can you hear me?''

''Yes…'' The word hissed from her like a summer-sigh kind of breeze.

''Where are you? What do you see?''

''Us.'' A smile curved her lips, a smile that warmed his blood. ''We're making love.''

A part of him reveled in the success so far of their

little experiment and another part of him felt desire swoop through him as she released a throaty moan.

He remembered that moan from when they'd made love and the memory seared him. He mentally shook himself, knowing how important it was that he stay focused on their ultimate goal.

He knew the moment the scene in her mind changed. She drew a swift intake of breath and her face tightened with tension...with fear.

"Alyssa, talk to me. Tell me where you are, what you see." He felt her fear wafting from her in waves. It filled him up, tensing his muscles as he saw the terror and fear that twisted her features. "Alyssa...where are you?"

"Beneath a tree...with you."

"Tell me about the tree. What does it look like?" Even as he asked her this, he wondered if it was possible for her to slow the action in the vision, to focus on a single item rather than allowing the scene to play out to completion.

"It's twisted and gnarled...I've seen it before..."

"Where? Where have you seen it? In the park? At somebody's house?"

"No...not in the park...I...I can't remember...I don't know. Oh, help me... I'm on top of you now, straddling your waist and I feel the knife in my hand."

"Tell me about the knife," he said frantically as she tossed restlessly, her head moving back and forth as if to shake the vision from her mind. "Alyssa...the knife. Focus on the knife, just the knife."

She stilled, a frown furrowing her forehead. ''The knife,'' she repeated softly. ''The handle is carved... black, I think...no...blue...dark blue. The blade is razor sharp and about five inches long.'' She began to toss her head once again. ''No,'' she cried out.

''Look at the hands that hold the knife,'' Nick said urgently. ''Whose hands are they, Alyssa? Whose hands do you see?''

''Red. I see red.'' A sob choked from her. ''And now the knife...it's stabbing you and there's blood... so much blood. Nick...oh, Nick, you're dead. You're dead. And you deserved what you got, you bastard...just like all the others.''

Nick flung himself back against his chair in shock. The last sentence sounded as if it had come from another person's throat. Deep and harsh and filled with rage, the voice sent an icy chill up Nick's spine as he realized he'd just heard the killer's thoughts.

''Alyssa?'' He cleared his throat to chase away the touch of fear he heard in his own voice. ''Honey... where are you now?''

There was no reply, nor did she move at all. Nick called her name one more time and still she didn't respond. Apparently she was in the darkness of unconsciousness that seemed to follow her visions.

He knew it would be a few minutes before she resurfaced and he stood, too restless to sit next to her as he thought of what they'd just done, what he'd just learned.

He paced the room from one end to the other. And

what had he learned? That if her vision came true, he would meet his end from a sharp knife with a carved dark blue handle beneath a misshapen tree?

He couldn't believe that Alyssa would wield the knife that would take his life, so who? And why hadn't her vision shown him grabbing his gun and protecting himself? Why would he allow himself to be totally vulnerable to a killer?

There had to be more to it than what she was seeing, or a different interpretation of the events. Frustration, raw and greedy, gnawed at him.

He should be feeling a certain element of success at what they'd managed to accomplish. She'd managed to interact with him while her vision was taking place. Instead, he felt only more frustrated than before because he hadn't gotten enough information to figure out the identity of the killer.

Stopping his pacing, he gazed at her, wondering how long she'd be unconscious. Last time it hadn't been that long, but already the minutes seemed to be stretching into a worrisome length of time.

"And you deserved what you got, you bastard."

The words reverberated in his head, causing a chill inside him that he couldn't quite shake. They had been delivered with such strength, with such malice and self-righteousness.

What would make somebody believe he deserved to be stabbed to death? And what about the other victims?

Again he looked at her, his worry deepening as she remained so still. She'd been under too long…what if their little experiment had driven her so deep inside herself she never again surfaced?

They had no idea how the mind and body would react to such things. Wake up, Alyssa. He mentally willed her to open her eyes and be okay. Besides, this experiment hadn't really brought concrete answers, rather it only brought more questions.

With a sigh of relief, he hurried back to his chair by the side of the sofa as Alyssa moaned faintly.

"Alyssa? Are you all right?"

Her eyelids fluttered, then remained open, but they held the horror of her vision. Tears fell as she sat up. He moved next to her on the sofa and took her into his arms.

She wrapped her arms around his neck and clung to him as if he was her lifeline to sanity. Her body was cold, her skin pale and clammy and her heart beat like that of a frightened bird held in his hands.

She cried only a brief time, then moved out of his arms, as if sorry for the show of momentary weakness. "Are you all right?" he asked as she stood.

She nodded. "I'm fine."

She didn't look fine to him. She still appeared unusually pale and shaken. "Do you remember everything that just happened?"

She reached up with one hand and twirled the bottom ends of a strand of hair between her fingers. "I remember. It was strange. I felt like I was living in the vision and yet I also knew that I was on the sofa and you were next to me, talking to me. Did anything

I said help?'' She leaned weakly against the back of the sofa.

Nick's worry about her increased. She seemed to be depleted of all energy, as if the vision had sucked the blood out of her. He didn't remember her looking so weak, so utterly spent the last time she'd had a vision.

''Why don't we head over to Ruby's and get a bite to eat?'' he asked impulsively, thinking the fresh air and some food might do her some good.

''Oh, I don't know...I need to...to...'' She frowned in bewilderment, as if she couldn't believe that there was nothing she needed to do.

He sensed her withdrawing from him, as if preparing to distance herself emotionally and physically. He couldn't allow her to do that, not now, not after what she'd just been through.

''You don't need to do anything but come have a late dinner with me.'' He took her by the elbow and propelled her toward the doorway.

She resisted for a moment, then seemed to relent and together they left the bed-and-breakfast. Ruby's lights gleamed through the trees of the park, but instead of cutting through the square, they stuck to the sidewalk.

He let her set their walking pace, and she moved slowly, laboriously, as if still weak and exhausted from what she'd just experienced.

Nick cursed himself for pushing her, for wanting...needing her to try to ''see'' something that might help the investigation. He knew how much the vision upset her and he should have never encouraged her to welcome it into her mind.

"I'm sorry," he said.

"For what?"

"For making you do that."

She smiled, but the gesture didn't quite reach her eyes. "It was my decision. You have nothing to apologize for. I'm just sorry it didn't help."

"It might have helped. I'm still working everything around in my mind." He fell silent as they reached Ruby's door.

The café was surprisingly busy for the lateness of the hour. Two tables had been pushed together to accommodate a group of older people who appeared to have just come from a square dance. The men were clad in jeans and western shirts and the ladies wore short dresses in bright colors over petticoats.

Nick and Alyssa chose a table near the back, away from the raucous group. Ruby took their orders, obviously pleased to see the two of them together.

"Are you sure you're all right?" Nick asked once Ruby had left them alone.

"I'm okay." The haunted darkness in her eyes belied her words. "It's just…it gets more and more difficult to come back to reality each time I have the vision."

"Have you had ones like this one before—ones that come persistently and leave you so wrung out?"

"No, and that's what scares me about this one." She toyed with the salt and pepper shakers in the center of the table, moving them from one place to another. He couldn't help noticing her hands trembled slightly. "Have you found out anything about Michael's murder? You said earlier today that it was different from the rest."

"Different in that he was still clothed, but the medical examiner thinks he was killed by the same type of knife as the others."

"So, what does that mean?" It was obvious she wanted something to keep her mind off the vision she'd just experienced. He wasn't sure that talking about a murder would do the trick, but it seemed to be her choice of conversation.

"We don't know for sure what it means. It's possible the killer was interrupted before Michael could be stripped naked. Or it's possible he was killed for a reason different from the others. The level of malevolence in his stabbing is also different from the others. Michael was only stabbed twice. The others were stabbed multiple times. Again, it's possible that the killer was interrupted, and if the crime had played out to its entirety, Michael would have been left exactly like the others."

Nick stopped talking as Ruby returned to their table with their orders. The big woman visited with them for a moment, making small talk, then left them to enjoy their food.

For a few minutes they ate in silence, and Nick found himself once again playing and replaying every detail of her vision in his head.

"The tree you see in your vision? You said it

seemed familiar. You still can't place where you've seen it before?''

''No. I've thought about it a hundred times, but I can't remember.'' She picked the onions off her burger with her fork. ''What do you think the tree means?''

''I don't know. Maybe the tree is in the yard of the killer. Maybe it's a tree that means something significant to him.''

She took a bite of her hamburger and chewed thoughtfully, then gazed at him, her eyes still holding that haunted look that made him want to grab her and hold her tight. ''Somehow, in my mind, I'm connecting with the killer, aren't I?''

''I believe so.''

She popped a French fry into her mouth, that endearing frown creasing her forehead. ''What I don't understand is why the killer would believe you deserve to die, that all the victims so far have deserved what they've gotten.''

''If this is some sort of vigilante motive due to the fact that three of the men had a reputation for being womanizers and the killer knew that Greg cheated on Virginia, no stretch of anyone's imagination can put me in that same category,'' he said.

''I just wish I could have been more helpful. Maybe when we go back to the bed-and-breakfast we should try it again.''

''No. We're not going to do that. Besides, it's possible you helped more than you know. If you really are connecting with the serial killer, then I now know what the murder weapon looks like.''

''That it has a dark blue handle.''

He nodded. ''And something else you said has been working around in my head.''

''What's that?''

''When I asked you to focus on the hands that you saw in your vision, you said you saw red, then you said the knife stabbed me and there was blood. But you saw the red before you saw the blood.''

''I remember.'' She ate another fry, her gaze focused on some point in the center of the table. ''But now I can't remember what I meant. Maybe the hands holding the knife were red?''

Nick nodded. ''Maybe chapped, or work-worn hands.''

They fell silent once again and focused on the rest of their meal. Nick was pleased to see the color slowly returning to her face and that she nearly finished all the food that was on her plate.

She finally pushed her plate aside and once again gazed at him. ''You do this all the time, don't you?''

''Do what?''

''Try to get into the mind of killers.''

''That's my job, that's what I've been trained to do,'' he explained.

''How do you do it? Dwell in the darkness of a killer's mind over and over again and remain sane?''

He finished the last French fry on his plate, then wiped his mouth on the paper napkin. ''I got some very good advice from a commanding officer when I first went into profiling.''

"And what was that?" she asked.

"He told me that for every moment I spent in the darkness, dwelling in the twisted minds of killers, I should spend an equal amount of time in a happy, sane place." He reached across the table and took her hand in his. "And during the time I've been here…delving into the darkness, you have become my happy, sane place."

The expression in her eyes was a curious blend of pleasure and pain. She tightened her fingers around his. "Let's go, Nick. I need a happy, sane place tonight."

Chapter 12

You have become my happy, sane place.

Nobody had ever said anything as wonderful as the words Nick had said to her as they finished their meal. She knew as they walked, hand in hand, back to the bed-and-breakfast, that they were going to make love again.

She could feel it in the warmth of Nick's hand holding hers, felt it in his gaze when he looked at her. They were going to make love again and he would be her happy, sane place, too.

"You will be alone," her grandmother had told her. "Your gift will make it so. You will eventually learn to accept your place in life...your aloneness, your separation from all others." The words whirled around and around in her head as they walked, bringing with them a warning that, at the moment, Alyssa didn't want to hear.

Tomorrow, v-gi-li-si...tomorrow, my grandmother, I will be alone. Or next week, or next year...but tonight she would be in Nick's arms. Tonight she would not be alone.

When they entered the back door Virginia met them in the foyer. "Oh, there you are," she said to Alyssa. "I was wondering where everyone was." She wrapped her arms around her shoulders. "I was spooked here all alone."

"We just went to get a bite to eat at Ruby's," Nick said.

"Oh..." Virginia's gaze shifted from Nick to Alyssa, then back to Nick again and her eyes widened slightly. Alyssa knew the woman was just now recognizing that there might be something more than a guest-hostess relationship between Alyssa and Nick. "Well, now that I know I'm not alone in the house anymore, I can go upstairs and sleep peacefully. Good night to you both," she said.

Nick and Alyssa waited in the small foyer until she had climbed the stairs and disappeared into her room, then Nick led Alyssa upstairs to his room.

They didn't speak a word. No words were needed. They undressed, then each slid beneath the sheets on the bed and they came together and formed a tangled knot of warm skin as their mouths sought connection.

As always, the taste of his lips thrilled her, the feel of his skin against her own quickened her heartbeat and sent a swirling wealth of desire through her.

A tiny piece of horror from the vision had lingered through their meal, but it couldn't continue to exist while she was being held in Nick's strong arms. His fevered kiss banished the horror, driving it away beneath a mastery of sweet sensations.

There was no room for thoughts of murder in the bed. There was no room for anything but Nick. As his hands moved down to cup her breasts, she moaned in utter abandon, giving herself to him not only in body, but in mind, as well.

His hands fired heat into her, warming all the places inside her that had been so cold...so frightened. And he followed the path of his hands with his mouth, taking first one of her nipples in his mouth, then the other.

She tangled her hands in his hair, wanting to pull him closer...closer still...close enough that they somehow melded together in a oneness that nothing could separate.

All her internal defenses tumbled down and she let them, knowing she could trust Nick as she'd trusted no other person in her life. She cried out his name, unable to think of anything but him as he drew her closer and closer to climax.

She stiffened and moaned as sweet, shuddering sensations consumed her. At the same time, he moved on top of her and his mouth once again found hers in a kiss that stole whatever breath might have been left in her body.

She was still riding the last of the waves of pleasure when he entered her. In one smooth long stroke, he refired her desire for more...more.

Hungrily, desperately, she moved her hips, thrusting upward to meet him. Nick…Nick…his name, his essence, his very being filled her body, her head and heart.

"Alyssa," he whispered as he took possession of her over and over again. "Sweet Alyssa, you take my breath away."

"Yes." It was the only word she could form as she was lost in a bewitching haze of his making, a mist of pleasure that obscured everything else.

The first time they'd made love had been slow, controlled. This time was different. He came at her with a desperate kind of hunger that stirred a frantic need in her.

Faster and faster they thrust together, their gasps and moans filling the room along with the moonlight that streamed in through the window.

Alyssa knew the moment he was about to lose control. His heartbeat crashed against her own and every muscle in his body tensed. She tightened her legs around him, wanting to draw him in deeper. With a deep, hoarse groan, he stiffened against her as he gained his release.

Afterward they remained wrapped together, a tangle of arms and legs beneath the cocoon of the sheet. Nick's hand smoothed across her hair. She couldn't remember the last time she'd felt so much at peace, the last time her mind was so quiet and she'd been so utterly relaxed.

But she could tell Nick didn't feel the same kind of peace that she did. Even though his hand gently stroked her hair, she felt a tension radiating from him that belied the easy caress.

She didn't have to be a psychic to know that although physically he was beside her in the bed, mentally he'd gone someplace else. He'd left his happy, sane place and had gone back to the darkness.

She placed a hand on his heart, feeling the steady beat beneath the warm skin. "Where are you, Nick?" she asked softly.

His chest moved up and down on a deep sigh. "Lost," he replied with an edge of frustration in his voice.

She changed positions so that her arms were across his chest and her chin rested on her arms. The moonlight splashed across his features, emphasizing the lines and planes that formed a handsome face. She knew where he was lost…in the crimes that remained unsolved.

"Do you want me to try again? Go into the vision and see if we can learn anything more?"

"Absolutely not," he replied. He placed his arm around her back, as if protecting her from herself and her offer.

"Then talk to me," she said. "Tell me what you're thinking."

He smiled ruefully. "Trust me, you don't want to share my thoughts."

"But I do," she protested. She wanted every piece of him she could get before he left her life for good.

He raised one arm up over his head, a frown furrowing across his forehead and deepening the starbursts of fine lines at the corners of his eyes. "I was just thinking about our bad guy."

"The man who possibly has red hands."

"If you're right about the red hands, then it's somebody who probably works outside," he continued thoughtfully.

"That doesn't narrow the field much. Most of the men around here are farmers and ranchers. They probably all have reddened work-worn hands."

His chest rose and fell once again in another deep sigh. "Something else I find intriguing is the fact that not one of the victims had any defensive wounds at all. What does that tell you about the crimes?"

"Probably the same things it tells you," she replied. "That they either knew the killer and had no reason to fear themselves in danger, or they somehow never saw it coming."

"There's no way they didn't see it coming. I figure it had to be somebody who appeared to pose no physical threat."

She ran her hand through his wiry chest hair, loving the way it curled around her fingers as she slid them through the thick patch. "Wasn't it Ted Bundy who used to pose like someone with a broken leg so women wouldn't think he was a threat when he approached them?"

He eyed her with surprise. "Very good. So, you know anyone around town who is pretending to have a broken leg or some sort of injury that would be nonthreatening?"

"Nobody comes to mind."

"Yeah, I didn't think it would be that easy." He reached out and ran his fingers lightly across her mouth. "When this is all over, why don't you blow this joint and come to Tulsa."

Although her heart quickened at his words, she knew better than to allow herself to share in any fantasy he might be spinning while she lay naked in his arms.

She laughed. "I'm not sure I'm ready to let Ruby have her wicked ways with my bed-and-breakfast." She kept her tone light as if she'd taken his words as a joke.

He pulled her closer and she placed her head on his chest, his heartbeat strong and reassuring beneath her ear. As he stroked her hair once again, she closed her eyes.

Alone. Her grandmother's voice seemed to whisper in her ear. *It is the destiny of ones who have the vision to remain alone.*

Those words echoing in her head, in her heart, served as a heart-wrenching lullaby as she drifted off to sleep.

Alyssa sat at her kitchen island sipping from a glass of iced tea and studying her finances. It had been three weeks since Michael Stanmeyer's murder, three weeks that she hadn't accepted a guest into the house other than Virginia.

It had taken several days for the police to release the room, then another couple of days for Alyssa to pack up Michael's personal belongings and send them to a relative in California.

Nick had told her she was welcome to resume the normal activities of the bed-and-breakfast, but she'd canceled any new guests for the next month and had Mary working the ice-cream parlor in the evenings.

For the past three weeks, her life had fallen into a new kind of pattern, one that revolved around Nick and the murders.

Already the police were concerned that the time for yet another murder was drawing closer, that whatever timetable the killer seemed to be keeping would force him to act again soon.

Her days were spent puttering around the place, doing chores and tasks she hadn't had time to do before. During the evenings, despite Nick's reluctance to the contrary, she consciously entered the vision that she still felt held the clue to the killer's identity.

Each time, Nick sat beside her, asking her questions, trying to delve deeper and deeper into the mist of her mind to retrieve any information that might be helpful. Afterward they went to Ruby's for dinner, then back to the bed-and-breakfast and into Nick's bed.

She didn't give herself time to consider if she was being a fool, making love to Nick night after night and knowing there was no future for them together. She merely took each moment with him as a gift to herself.

A rapid knock on the front door pulled her from her glass of iced tea and through the living room. She unlocked the door and opened it to see her aunt Rita, Savannah and Breanna standing there.

"What's this? A family reunion?" She hugged each of them, holding on tight for a moment longer than necessary to each of her family members.

"We just decided it was time for a visit, just us women," Savannah said as Alyssa ushered them into the kitchen.

"I'm so glad you did. Sit down. How about some iced tea?"

"Iced tea sounds wonderful," Rita said as she fanned her face with her hand. "No living creature should be out in this heat," she exclaimed. She smiled as Alyssa placed the cold drink before her. "Thank you, dear."

There were no lingering signs of the trauma Rita had gone through while kidnapped and held captive by a madman. Her short dark hair was perfectly coiffed and her dark eyes radiated with her love of life.

"Breanna, you're looking absolutely gorgeous," Alyssa said.

"I'm getting fat," Breanna replied.

Alyssa squeezed her cousin's shoulder as she placed a drink before her. "But it's the best kind of fat…baby fat."

Breanna stroked her burgeoning tummy and her smile of satisfaction sent a whisper of wistfulness through Alyssa. What must it be like? To carry the child of the man you love inside your belly?

She would never know, for her destiny was a life alone, without a husband, without children.

"You should see Adam," Savannah said as she raked a hand through her short black hair. The short hair emphasized her high cheekbones and lovely eyes. "The man acts as if he's the only being on earth who has ever made a baby."

"He acts just like your Riley does," Breanna protested.

They all laughed and a sudden melancholy brought unexpected, unwelcome tears to Alyssa's eyes. Horrified, she quickly swiped at them, but not before Rita saw her.

"What is it, my little one?" Rita pulled out the chair next to her and forced Alyssa to sit, then she wrapped an arm around her shoulder.

"Nothing…I…I don't know." Embarrassment forced a burst of uncomfortable laughter from her. "I'm just so glad you all stopped by for a visit."

"When I spoke to you yesterday you sounded more stressed than I'd ever heard you. We came by to make sure you were doing okay," Rita said.

"I'm fine." Alyssa forced a smile to reassure them. She knew exactly what it was that had forced the tears to her eyes. It was knowing that her two "sisters" had found true love, were starting families and living the kind of life Alyssa would never experience.

"You aren't fine. What's going on?" Savannah asked. "More visions?"

Alyssa hadn't shared her latest vision, the one about Nick and the murders, with her family. She did so now, although she kept the part where she and Nick made love to herself. But she told them about the tree, about the knife and the horror of stabbing somebody over and over again.

"Nick and I have been trying to get details from the vision," she explained. "I've been consciously willing them to come to me, trying to dissect from them anything that might help identify the killer."

"Oh, Alyssa…that sounds troubling," Savannah said. "I hate the idea of you having visions on purpose."

"The killer is leaving precious few clues for the authorities. Somebody has to do something to stop the murders."

"I've heard you're seeing quite a bit of Nick," Rita said, her gaze sharp on the niece she'd raised as one of her own daughters. "The word is, you two have been spotted most nights looking quite cozy at Ruby's."

"I told you, I'm helping with the investigation." Alyssa reached up for a strand of her hair, then realizing what she was doing, dropped her hand back to her lap.

"Oh, so it's strictly a business relationship," Breanna said with a sly smile.

Alyssa's cheeks warmed. "He's a nice man." The words sounded utterly lame and the heat of her blush intensified.

"Working on the investigation must agree with you," Rita said, her gaze still intent on Alyssa's features. "There's a look about you I've never seen before."

"Must be stress," Alyssa joked.

"Hmm," Rita replied with a small smile.

They remained for a little over an hour, talking about things that brought a measure of relaxation to Alyssa.

Breanna spoke of her six-year-old daughter, Maggie, telling stories that had them all in fits of laughter. Savannah talked about her new life in Sycamore Ridge, a town about an hour's drive away, and Rita spoke of the fall festival that would be taking place at the Cherokee Cultural Center in the next couple of days.

It was a pleasant respite from the darkness that had seemed to inch closer and closer around Alyssa for the last couple of weeks.

Their company was also a reminder that no matter what, she would never be utterly alone, that she would always have the love and support of her family. This thought gave her a renewed burst of inner strength.

She felt better...stronger as she told them all goodbye. Savannah and Breanna went out to the car, but Alyssa's aunt lingered behind for a moment.

"You've built a fine business here, Alyssa," she said as the two stood on the front porch of the bed-and-breakfast. "Your uncle Thomas and I are very proud of you."

"That's always been important to me," Alyssa said. "That I make you proud. I have no other way to repay you for all the love you gave to me when I needed it most."

Rita's dark eyes smiled before the gesture touched

her lips. "You were an easy child to love, my dear, and now you're all grown up and should be looking outside your family for a different kind of love."

"I…" The protest that Alyssa was about to speak was silenced as her aunt placed a finger to her lips.

"Don't speak, just listen. If this man, this Nick, fulfills you as a woman, then trust what's in your heart, not whatever visions might be in your head." She dropped her finger from Alyssa's mouth and sighed.

"I had plenty of time to think when I was in that basement room as Jacob Kincaid's prisoner. I faced all the fears that a mother could face when she thought she was on the verge of death. And the one fear I had was that my children wouldn't know the kind of love that I've known with your uncle Thomas. In the end, love is the only legacy we leave behind."

She didn't wait for Alyssa's reply, but instead turned and left the porch to meet her daughters at her car.

Alyssa watched as her family members drove away, her aunt's words ringing in her ears. Alyssa knew she was in love with Nick.

She had no idea when it had happened, how she had allowed him so deep into her heart, into the bruised soul of her being. But he was there, filling up the spaces that had been empty all her life, accepting her visions without judgment, without fear, simply as part of her.

But as deep as he'd burrowed into her heart, she had no idea what place she had in his. Each night they delved into the darkness of her vision, then sought the light in each other's arms, making love with a frantic need, a desperate desire to banish the darkness forever.

She knew he cared about her, knew he wanted her. But he hadn't again mentioned her leaving Cherokee Corners for Tulsa. They had talked about anything and everything in their lives except a future.

Not that she expected a future with him. Even a handsome, caring man like Nick couldn't change the patterns of life that fate had laid out, and Alyssa knew the trail of her life was one she would walk alone.

She drew a deep breath. There was a storm coming. She could feel it in the humid, soupy air, smell the hint of wildness in the atmosphere. Despite the muggy heat that surrounded her, an inexplicable chill crept up her back. She turned and went back into the house and carefully locked the door behind her.

Chapter 13

"Jason Sheller," Nick said the name and watched Clay's reaction. The two men were alone in the war room, the others having left for the night moments earlier.

"What about him?" Clay asked.

"What do you know about him?"

Clay shrugged. "He's been in Cherokee Corners for the past four years...transferred here from someplace down in Texas. Why?"

"From Dallas. He transferred from the Dallas police force." Nick frowned down at the paperwork in front of him, then looked back at Clay. "What else do you know about him?"

"Not a lot. He seems to be a decent cop, but he's kind of a loner. I get the impression he was a little fish in a big pond in Dallas and hoped that here he could be a big fish in a smaller pond."

"So, he's ambitious?"

"Definitely. What are you thinking?"

Nick sighed and shut the file folder before him. "I don't know. I'm grasping at straws. Sheller just gives me an uncomfortable feeling. It seems like whenever I turn around he's right under my nose."

Clay laughed. "He is a pain in the ass. I think he really wanted to be a part of the task force, probably saw it as a stepping stone to advance his career, but I don't think he's hiding any deep, dark secrets."

"Somebody is, dammit." Nick raked a hand through his hair in frustration. "We've been here a month and we're no closer to catching the killer than we were on the day we arrived."

"That doesn't necessarily speak to our incompetence, but rather to the adroitness of the killer," Clay replied.

Nick flashed him a quick grin. "Thanks, I needed to hear that we aren't complete dunces."

"We're only as good as the clues left behind and this perp isn't leaving behind much of anything for us to go on."

Nick heard his own frustration reflected in Clay's tone. They were all feeling the rancor of failure, the pressure of defeat where this killer was concerned.

To complicate matters, for the past two days tourists had been pouring into town for the fall festival at the cultural center.

The police department was stretched thin and Chief Cleberg was terrified the next victim would be a hapless tourist.

"I guess we might as well call it a night," Nick said reluctantly. "We aren't accomplishing much anyway."

"He'll make a mistake, Nick." Clay rose from the table where they had been seated. "Sooner or later he's going to make a mistake. It's just a matter of time."

"Yeah, but how many more victims are there going to be before that mistake is made?"

It was a rhetorical question and Clay didn't attempt to answer. "I'm going to check a few things in the lab. I'll see you in the morning."

Nick nodded, but remained seated at the table. He rubbed his forehead where a headache had pounded with almost nauseating intensity for the past hour.

Something had to give…something had to break. He rose from the table and went to the single small window in the room. He peered outside where darkness had fallen unusually early. A brewing storm shot occasional streaks of lightning in the southwestern sky.

Rain would be a welcome relief from the dry conditions. Hopefully it would bring with it cooler temperatures. He looked at his watch. After eight. If Alyssa hadn't already eaten, he'd take her to Ruby's for a late-night supper.

Alyssa. He'd never been so damn confused about a woman before. His relationship with Dorrie had been incredibly easy. They had met, fallen in love and married. With Alyssa nothing was easy although everything felt right.

He'd met her and he'd fallen in love with her. There were moments when he reveled in the love that filled his heart for her, and other moments when he despaired.

No matter how often they had made love, no matter how many thoughts and feelings they had shared, he sensed that there was a tiny piece of herself she held back.

Selfishly he wanted to breach that private place, storm her defenses and tumble that wall that he thought still existed between them.

On the other hand, he wondered if perhaps out of all the people in the world, they were the two who should not be together. She had a darkness in her from her visions, was acutely tuned in to the shadows of evil.

He was a man who worked with that evil, who wrapped it around him like a second skin and brought that darkness home with him each night.

Was it fair for him to want her to share that kind of life with him? Knowing that by his work alone he might cause her more pain and more horrendous visions of death?

He loved her. He loved her enough to do the right thing even if the right thing was to walk away from her and let her live in relative peace.

The thought of her not in his life, not in his future ached inside him, but if by being with her he brought more pain, more darkness into her life, then he'd learn to live without her.

But he wasn't out of her life yet and suddenly he

was eager to get to the bed-and-breakfast and see her beautiful face, talk to her about inconsequential pleasures and joys.

Tonight he would insist she not pull up the vision, not put herself through the agony of seeing that terrible scene in her mind. Tonight they wouldn't talk of murders or death.

Eager now to leave, he locked up the war room and headed down the hallway toward the front of the station. If he hurried he and Alyssa could get to Ruby's, eat and get home before the storm broke loose.

"Agent Mead." The desk officer, Corey Sinclair, stopped him before he could exit the building. "I've got something here for you." He held out a small white envelope.

"What's this?" Nick asked as he took the envelope from the man.

"Beats me," Officer Sinclair replied. "If I was to guess, it looks like some sort of invitation to a party." He grinned. "There's plenty of single women in this town who wouldn't mind throwing a party just to get you invited."

Nick tore open the envelope and removed the small card. It wasn't an invitation. The words *Thinking of You* were just below the picture of a grinning cat. Nick's heart warmed. Alyssa, he thought. She must have dropped the card by at some point during the day.

He opened the card and the warmth that had momentarily suffused him froze in an icy river that ran through his veins. His eyes glanced over the inane preprinted message to the handwritten words below it. GOOD TO SEE YOU AGAIN, NICK. And the signature was a single letter, a familiar M.

Murphy. The name screamed through Nick.

"Who delivered this?" he demanded of Officer Sinclair as his gaze shot around the room.

"I don't know. It was here when I came on duty a little while ago."

"I need to know how this got here…who delivered it." He slammed his hand down on the counter. "Dammit, somebody must have seen something. I want some answers now! I'm taking this to the lab, and I'll be right back."

With the roar of fear…and rage ringing in his ears, Nick carried the card back to the lab where Clay was still working. "I need you to fingerprint this right away." He held the card out before him with two fingers, cursing the fact that he'd already gotten his own prints on the card and envelope.

Clay pulled on a set of gloves and took the items from Nick. "Something to do with our case?"

"Something to do with an old case." Nick felt scattered to the winds, watching impatiently as Clay set to dusting the card and envelope.

Murphy. Here in Cherokee Corners. The shock of seeing that familiar initial still ripped through him. He'd hoped the man dead, or at least in prison. His hands clenched and unclenched at his sides. But he was here…in this town, and Nick wanted him… wanted him badly.

"What's going on?" Chief Cleberg appeared in the

doorway. "Officer Sinclair said you're upset about something."

"A card was here for me. It's from the man who killed my wife. I want to know how it got here, how it was delivered, if any officer got a look at whoever brought it in." The words shot from Nick with the force of bullets.

"I don't see anything here but what is probably your fingerprints," Clay said and looked up from his work.

Frustration raged through Nick even though he'd expected exactly what Clay had just told him. Murphy was far too smart to leave fingerprints behind.

"I'll check to see if anyone saw who brought the card in," Cleberg said. "But the station has been busy today…lot of people in and out. I checked with Officer Bledlow, who was on duty before Sinclair, and he said he doesn't remember anything on the desk addressed to you. It must have been brought in during shift change."

Nick nodded, knowing that the man he sought would have used the cover of others to drop off the card. Or he would have paid some kid to deliver the card.

Memories crashed through his head… Dorrie in that damn motel room. The painting on the wall splashed with her lifeblood. The M carved into her chest.

The horror…the pain…the rage all boiled inside him as powerful, as sickening as if visiting him for the first time.

"Nick...are you okay?" Clay's voice penetrated the fog that had wrapped itself around Nick's brain.

"No...no, I'm not fine," he said unevenly. Memories continued to attack him...memories he didn't want, ones that he'd hoped he'd forever forgotten. The tangy unmistakable odor of blood...the splayed bright blond hair against the pillow...the horrible expressions on the faces of his fellow officers.

Then a new image presented itself to him...the image of Alyssa in a motel room, her black hair spread out on the pillow beneath her head...her dark blue eyes staring but unseeing.

Alyssa!

The thought of her and the potential danger she could be in forced a burst of adrenaline through him. "I've got to go," he said to the two men who had been watching him.

He didn't wait to make further explanations, his only need was to get to Alyssa now...immediately. He raced from the lab down the hallway to the front door.

He burst out into the night that smelled of the impending storm. Hot wind whipped around him as he ran to his car, his heart thrashing a rhythm of panic.

The air crackled with electricity and the hint of unbridled wildness. But nothing nature could conjure up could compete with the wildness that raced through Nick.

Murphy had taken one woman he loved from him. Nick wasn't willing to give up another one. He started the engine of his car and jammed it into gear, leaving

an inch of rubber from his wheels as he peeled out
of the station parking lot and down the street to the
city square.

Where was he? Where was Murphy? Was he in a
car behind him, following him to the bed-and-
breakfast? How long had he been in town? Did he
know who Nick's friends were?

Did he know about Alyssa?

Did he know that Nick cared about her?

He slammed the car into park in front of the bed-
and-breakfast and ran to the front door. Locked. He
banged on it with his fist, hoping that she would hear
him and open it.

When he'd banged three times and nobody came
to the door, he raced around the building to the back,
fumbling for his keys as he ran. Once there, he unlocked the door and flew inside.

"Alyssa!"

No answer. Frustration battling with fear, he
knocked on the door to her private quarters. Still no
reply. Where the hell could she be?

"Alyssa?" This time he yelled her name up the
stairs, following his voice by taking the stairs two at
a time. Virginia's door was closed and Alyssa wasn't
in any of the other rooms.

He crashed a fist against Virginia's door, where
loud music seeped beneath the wooden barrier.
"Come in," she called out.

He opened the door to see her seated near the window painting her fingernails while a small stereo unit

blared one of the latest hits of a country-western group.

"Nick!" She jumped up from her chair and blew on scarlet fingernails. "I thought you were Alyssa. What's going on?"

"Where is Alyssa?"

"Why? What's going on?"

"Nothing. Nothing is going on. Where is she? Do you know?" Even though he tried to keep the urgency out of his voice, he heard the strident tones of panic.

"She went over to Ruby's to get something to eat. Are you going to tell me what's going on?" she asked impatiently.

"I told you, nothing is going on." He had no time for explanations or chitchat. As he turned he was aware of Virginia grabbing her purse, and as he headed back down the stairs, he heard her following after him.

He left the bed-and-breakfast, but instead of taking the sidewalk around to Ruby's he cut through the park. Ruby's lights gleamed through the trees that whipped and tossed in the wind. Lightning streaked the sky, followed seconds later by a crack of thunder.

She has to be there, he thought as he hurried toward the café. She has to be there safe and sound. And he had to figure out what he was going to do.

Maybe Murphy just arrived in town today. Maybe he hadn't had time yet to know about Nick's personal habits or the connections he'd made with people while he'd been working here.

Maybe Murphy didn't know about Nick's personal connection to Alyssa, a connection Nick had to sever immediately. It might just save her life.

As he broke from the wooded path to cross the street, he immediately spied Alyssa at a table toward the back of the establishment. Relief fluttered through him, but it was a short-lived relief.

She was okay now, but he had to do something to make certain she continued to be okay. As he pushed open the door to the café he was vaguely aware of Virginia hurrying down the sidewalk toward the place.

Apparently he'd stirred her curiosity enough to get her out of her room and away from her fingernail painting. Well, she could just watch the show he was going to put on. The more spectators there were, the better. He could use the local gossips more now than ever before.

The look of pleasure that stole over Alyssa's features as she spied him sent a wave of sweet heat through him, but it wasn't enough to banish the chill that a single letter M had created inside him.

He knew his idea was a lame one, but at the moment it was the only idea he had and he hoped that later Alyssa would forgive him for what he was about to do.

"Hi, handsome." Ruby greeted him with a warm smile from behind the cash register.

"Hey, Ruby, how's it going?" He forced a light, easy tone as his gaze scanned the faces of the other diners. There weren't many and thankfully he saw no strangers.

''Good thing you didn't try to come in at dinner-time,'' she said. ''Had the biggest crowd I think we've ever served. I love hungry tourists. You'd better get on back there.'' She jerked a thumb in Alyssa's direction. ''I know she's waiting for you.''

He steeled himself as he approached the booth where Alyssa awaited him. It's a dumb idea, Mead, a small voice whispered inside his head. But desperation drove men to drastic measures and Nick had never felt so desperate in his life.

He couldn't warn her, couldn't tell her what he was going to do ahead of time. It had to look real…it had to be real. ''Hi,'' he said as he reached the booth.

''Hi yourself,'' she replied. ''The storm made me restless so I decided to come on over here and see if the wind eventually blew you in.''

Why did she have to look so damn pretty? Her hair was loose and flowing down her back and he wanted to wrap himself in it and get lost. She wore a beige sundress with blue embroidered flowers. The combination of beige and blue set off her beautiful skin tone and emphasized the deep blue of her eyes…eyes that at the moment had a quiet happiness he was about to shatter.

''Aren't you going to sit down?'' she asked.

''No, I just wanted to talk to you. I'm moving out of your place tonight.''

A frown furrowed the smoothness of her forehead as she gazed up at him in surprised bewilderment.

"Moving out? What do you mean? Has something happened? Is something wrong?"

He couldn't meet her gaze. He stared at a point just over the top of her head. "Nothing's happened and there's nothing wrong. I'm just feeling a little claustrophobic, is all." His voice was too loud and he knew he was drawing the attention of everyone in the place.

"Claustrophobic?" The furrow in her forehead deepened. "I...I don't understand."

"Look, Alyssa, we've had a good time together, but I'm not the kind of man to stick around anyplace or anyone for too long. You've shown me a good time, but it wasn't meant to be anything more."

If this didn't work out the way he'd planned, he wondered how many years he'd spend trying to forget the look she wore on her face at that very moment.

Chapter 14

Alyssa couldn't make sense of it. As she stared up at him, her mind tried to make sense of the words that were coming out of his mouth. This wasn't right. This wasn't Nick. He looked like Nick, smelled like Nick, but this wasn't the man she'd known for the last month.

She was conscious of the curious stares of the other people in the café and the heat of embarrassment burned in her cheeks. "Nick, would you please sit down and let's talk quietly about this."

"See, that's what I mean, sleep with a woman a couple of times and she thinks she owns you." His voice was still loud, too loud.

She felt as if she'd been slapped across the face and she couldn't help the hot sting of tears that burned in her eyes.

He looked around the café and laughed. "Small-town girls...you gotta love them. Too bad they have to take everything so seriously. Look, babe, we had a good time, but I've been worried that you're seeing something that isn't there between us. I mean, hell, you've been entertaining and all, but it's time for me to move on."

Embarrassment was nothing beneath the pain his callous words brought. Had she so badly misjudged the kind of man he was, the kind of relationship they had? She felt as if she were in a dream...no...a nightmare, but she wasn't waking up and it wasn't going away.

The burning in her eyes increased and she swallowed hard, knowing she would die if she allowed the tears to fall here in a public place.

"Well, you don't have to worry about it, Nick." She stood, shoulders rigid, chin high. "I'm seeing things quite clearly now. I'll have your final bill ready when you get back to the bed-and-breakfast."

"Thanks, babe, I appreciate it," he said.

Alyssa held on to her composure as she walked toward the front door of the café. She was vaguely aware of Ruby's sympathetic face at the register, but she didn't stop there. She'd pay for her dinner tomorrow. Ruby would understand.

She had to get outside, away from the stares that followed her, away from Nick before she lost all her composure and crumbled into a heap of emotion.

Alone, you will live your life alone. Her grandmother's words echoed and reechoed in her head as she stepped out of the door and into the wind-whipped night.

Even though she'd thought she'd prepared herself for the eventuality of Nick leaving her life, she hadn't been prepared for this. Nothing in her life, nothing in the time she'd spent with Nick could have prepared her for the emotionless, cruel dismissal he'd just given her.

She ran straight ahead onto the wooded path that would lead her directly to her home. She needed the privacy of her rooms to mourn the loss of Nick, a man she'd apparently desperately misjudged.

Tears half blinded her as she ran. Wind tore through the trees and they moved in a macabre dance of nature. She raced past a bench, where a lamp created a pool of light in the center of the park.

Lightning lit the night like a camera flash gone awry and thunder boomed overhead, but not before she heard Nick calling her name.

Despite her desire to the contrary, she slowed her pace and turned her head in his direction. What he'd said to her had been despicable, especially in view of an audience.

But, that's not Nick, her heart cried out. That wasn't the man she had come to know, grown to love, learned to trust. That man in the café had been a stranger, with stranger's eyes and a demeanor incongruent with the Nick she knew.

She saw him approaching the bench and at the same time saw Virginia catch up with him. Alyssa frowned. What was she doing here? The blonde grabbed his arm to halt his forward progress.

Torn between wanting the privacy of her room and curiosity, Alyssa froze, watching the interplay between Virginia and Nick. She wasn't that far away from them. She could see their features as they spoke, but the wind crashing through the trees made what they were saying to each other impossible to hear.

As she stood in the shadows of the trees, a sense of everything gone wrong filled her, along with a terrible foreboding.

The night was wrong, with the violent skies and thick atmosphere. The pounding in her head was wrong, as if a vision wanted control but refused to take her over.

And the man was all wrong. She knew in her head, in her heart, that something was wrong with Nick and he hadn't meant anything he'd said to her.

She stared at Nick and Virginia and warnings screamed in her head. It was wrong. It was all wrong. Virginia shouldn't be here. None of them should be here, in the park, in the storm.

Nick appeared to be trying to escape from Virginia, but she had hold of one of his arms and seemed to be pleading with him.

He finally managed to yank his arm from her grasp at the same time she opened her purse and a slash of lightning rent the night.

In the glare of that light, Alyssa saw Virginia's nails dark with color. Wrong! Wrong, her brain screamed.

Hands...hands gripping a knife...red...not red hands...red fingernail polish. A blue-handled knife gripped in slender, feminine hands...hands with red fingernail polish.

"Nick!" His name burst from her in terror, but a loud clap of thunder swallowed the sound.

Still, he turned in her direction and Alyssa watched in horror as Virginia's hand raised and steel flashed as she struck him in the back. It happened in the space of a heartbeat, so fast, so unexpected.

Nick reeled sideways and crashed into the bench. "No!" Alyssa screamed as he fell to the ground and Virginia raised the bloody knife once again.

Fear catapulted Alyssa forward...fear for Nick's life. She had no idea if he was dead or alive, but there was no way she was going to let Virginia touch him with that knife again.

Just as Virginia began to kneel over Nick's prone body, Alyssa slammed into her. Together the two women rolled into the grass, grappling in a life-and-death battle.

Alyssa managed to grab hold of both of Virginia's wrists and she slammed the hand that held the knife against the ground in an effort to make the woman drop the weapon.

"What are you doing?" she cried as she struggled to gain control of the knife.

"He deserved it," Virginia screamed, her pretty features contorted into a mask of rage Alyssa had never seen before. "I did it for you! I did it for every woman who's ever been used by a man.'' With a roar, Virginia bucked Alyssa off her and rolled away.

She rose with the knife still in hand as Alyssa scrambled to her feet. ''You should have run back to your safe little bed-and-breakfast world, Alyssa.''

Virginia circled her, getting closer, her eyes gleaming as wickedly as the razor-sharp knife. ''I can't let you leave here. You'll have to be the first female victim of the Shameless Slasher.''

She lunged forward but stopped suddenly, a look of utter surprise on her face as her thigh exploded in a burst of blood. With a cry of pain, she fell to the ground, the knife spilling out of her hand.

Alyssa hadn't heard gunfire that had sent the bullet that ripped through Virginia's leg, but she turned to see Nick propped up against the bench, gun in hand and face as pale as death.

''Nick!'' She ran to his side, sobs choking her as she knelt down beside him. The gun fell to his side as if he hadn't the energy to hold it another minute longer. ''Hang on, Nick. I'll get help,'' she cried. Blood. There was too much blood.

He grabbed her arm, his eyes dark and glazed with pain. ''Dumb idea...''

''Don't talk...save your strength. Help us!'' she screamed, hoping somebody, anybody, would hear her.

''Listen.'' Nick squeezed her arm. ''It...it wasn't about her...''

''Please, Nick, don't talk now,'' Alyssa exclaimed as tears chased down her cheeks. ''Somebody...

please! Help us.'' She reached behind him and pressed her hand against the blood that poured out of his wound. Too much blood.

Virginia moaned. "Help me. I'm bleeding to death," she cried. "It hurts! It hurts so much."

Nick was bleeding to death, Alyssa thought. She screamed again and nearly sobbed in relief as somebody answered her cry. "We're here!" she called. "Get the police. Get an ambulance! Hang on, Nick. Please…hang on."

It was her vision…the storm, the knife and Nick bleeding to death. "Stay with me, Nick," she cried. "Don't make the vision be true."

The rain finally came while Nick was in recovery. Alyssa stood at the window in the waiting room and watched the rain beating down.

The last several hours had been a nightmare. Thankfully, somebody had called the cops and Virginia was now in a room down the hall under arrest despite the injury that had required medical care.

By the time the ambulance had arrived for Nick, he'd been unconscious and hadn't regained consciousness when he'd been whisked out of her sight and through emergency-room doors.

"Hell of a night."

She turned to see Chief Cleberg entering the room. "Yes, it has been," she agreed and moved away from the window and to a nearby chair.

"Heard about the scene in the café." He sank down in the chair next to her. "Hell of a thing Nick did, drawing Virginia out like he did. Wonder how he knew what would set her off?"

"Is she going to be all right?" Alyssa asked, although at this point she really didn't care about Virginia's welfare. The woman was a murderer.

"She's going to be just fine, healthy enough to spend the rest of her life behind bars." Glen expelled a deep breath. "We've got a lot of sorting out to do here." A frown creased his broad forehead. "We've got to figure out where we dropped the ball, how she managed to stay beneath the radar for so long. You doing okay?"

Alyssa nodded. "Fine. I just can't believe what's happened. I can't believe she was under my roof all this time and I didn't suspect her being anything other than a grieving widow."

The chief stood, a weary cast to his shoulders. "You should go home, Alyssa. Nick's been pumped full of blood, stitched up with care, and the doctor says he'll most likely sleep for the rest of the night. He'll be glad to see you fresh and gorgeous in the morning. I'll have one of my men drive you home."

She was reluctant to leave without seeing Nick, without making sure with her own eyes that he was resting peacefully and out of danger. But she knew Glen was right. She should go home and get some sleep herself and be here in the morning when Nick woke up.

"Thanks, I appreciate it."

Minutes later she was in the back of a patrol car. The rain had let up to a light drizzle and there was no hint of the lightning and thunder that had earlier energized the skies.

"I can't believe all this was going on and I was out on the highway writing speeding tickets," Jason Sheller said with disappointment. "I wish I could have been in that park, maybe I could have saved Nick from being stabbed."

"I wish you would have been there, too," Alyssa replied. "It was awful," she said.

"From what I hear, if you hadn't been there, Nick would be dead. You're a brave woman," Jason said.

"Thanks, but I just did what I could." She stared out the window.

The storm had passed, just as her vision had come to fruition. She should have been feeling relief. Her vision had played out in its entirety and Nick wasn't dead. But, rather than relief, she felt a restlessness drumming through her veins.

I'll feel better tomorrow when I can see him, she thought. I'll feel better once I hear his voice and see the light shining from his eyes.

As Jason pulled up in front of her house, she had the impulse to tell him to take her back to the hospital, that she'd sleep in a chair so she could be there if Nick awoke before morning.

But she talked herself out of it, realizing that if he came to, the first people who would want to talk to him would be Glen and the other men on the task force.

"Thanks, Jason. I appreciate the ride." She got out

of the car and ran toward the front door, pulling her keys out of her pocket at the same time.

She unlocked the front door and stepped inside. Her eyes felt gritty from all the tears she'd shed and from sheer exhaustion. But the restless energy she'd noticed in the car still clung to her.

Maybe a nice hot cup of tea would relax her enough to sleep, she thought. She went into her private quarters and put a mug of water into the microwave, then sat at the small table while she waited for the water to heat.

It was no wonder she felt edgy. She'd been through a trauma. It still all seemed too huge to wrap her mind around. The scene at Ruby's, the horror in the park, her fear for Nick and the sudden realization that Virginia was the serial killer that had terrorized the town all whirled in her head.

No wonder it had been so easy for her to tap into the killer…the killer had been living beneath her roof. She tried to remember everything Virginia had ever told her about her life before coming to Cherokee Corners as Greg's wife, but there was precious little that Virginia had shared.

The microwave dinged and a moment later she sat at the table with a cup of tea, her mind still whirling with thoughts of the events that had taken place.

"It wasn't about her."

She frowned and sipped her tea. Wasn't that what Nick had said to her as he lay bleeding in her arms? But that didn't make sense. Maybe he'd already been half-delirious from loss of blood.

She finished her tea, rinsed the cup in the sink, then stretched with arms overhead. Maybe now she could sleep and be at the hospital first thing in the morning to see Nick.

For a moment she thought about going upstairs, about sliding beneath the sheets that smelled of Nick and sleeping in the bed where they'd made love a dozen times. He would be leaving Cherokee Corners once he was well enough. His job here was finished.

She would change the sheets on the bed, wash away the scent of him and prepare for new guests while he returned to his life in Tulsa.

Her head was too full at the moment to think about the painful absence that would be left behind. She'd allow herself to feel that pain later, when lonely nights brought back the beautiful time they'd shared together.

She opened her bedroom door and flipped on the light switch that turned on the small lamp by the side of the bed. She froze for a moment as the picture hanging over the bed captured her attention. She took a couple of steps toward the foot of the bed.

The tree. The gnarled tree from her vision was depicted in the painting. Funny that she hadn't placed it before this moment. Odd that it had had such a prominent place in the vision that had now played out and been resolved. Each time she'd had her vision, death had occurred beneath the tree.

A sound behind her startled her, but before she could whirl around, one hand clamped down on her mouth and the other grabbed around her waist and she was pulled tight against a hard-muscled body.

Fear ripped through her as she struggled against the iron hold. "Stop it...stand still," a deep male voice commanded.

Realizing her struggles to free herself were futile, she did as he asked and stilled. His mouth moved to within an inch of her ear. Hot breath on her neck...his arm like a band of steel around her...fingers biting into the flesh around her mouth...the taste of terror sharp and acrid in her mouth.

"We haven't been officially introduced yet, but I'm a friend of Nick's," he said. "Maybe he's mentioned me to you. My name is Murphy."

The name shot horror through her. Her vision, it hadn't just been about the park and Nick and Virginia. It had been a melange of what had happened earlier and what was happening right now.

It was all perfectly clear now. She was the one who was going to die beneath the gnarled tree.

Chapter 15

Nick swam up from the depths of darkness and into a world of pain. His right shoulder blade throbbed, pain shooting from the back clear through to his chest. But he welcomed the pain. It meant he was alive.

He opened his eyes and found himself in a darkened hospital room, an IV stuck into the back of his hand. Movement sent sharp pain through him, but he tried to shove beyond the pain and center his thoughts.

The park…and Virginia. Memories of what had happened shot through his head. Virginia stopping him as he ran after Alyssa, asking him why he'd been so mean, then him breaking loose from her and turning his back.

Initially, he'd thought Virginia had pounded him in the back with her fist, but within the space of a breath, he'd realized it was far more serious than a fist-pounding.

It had been as if she'd opened a valve and instantly all his energy, all his life force, had begun to drain. And the pain...the excruciating pain had rendered him mindless for long moments.

If it hadn't been for Alyssa... Alyssa! Her name screamed through his mind followed by another name—Murphy. Dear God. He hadn't gotten a chance to warn her. He'd passed out before he'd had an opportunity to warn anyone.

He sat up and groaned as pain ripped through his shoulder and a wave of dizziness momentarily assaulted him. He drew a deep breath, attempting to force away the pain and the fuzziness.

He had to get out of here. He had to get to Alyssa.

He yanked the IV out of his hand and swung his legs over the side of the bed, then waited for a new wave of dizziness to leave him.

He hit the nurse call button as he stood unsteadily on his feet. He'd just managed to yank off the hospital gown and pull on his jeans when a young nurse bustled in.

Her bright blue eyes widened in horror as she spied him struggling to get on his shoes. "Mr. Mead, what are you doing? Get back into bed. Oh, my, you've pulled out your IV." She wrung her hands, obviously not knowing what to do with him.

"Is Chief Cleberg here?" he asked, trying to shove away the gnawing pain in his shoulder, the throb of the IV site and his terror for Alyssa.

"No, the doctor sent everyone home. Please, get back into bed, Mr. Mead. You shouldn't be up."

"What's your name?" he asked.

"Marianne...but—"

"Marianne, I need your car keys." He held out a hand to her.

"What?" Her eyes were impossibly large.

"Do you have a car?" he asked impatiently. She nodded. "I need your keys now," he continued. "It's a matter of life and death."

"But...I—" She jumped as Nick grabbed her by the shoulders. "Marianne, honey. I don't have time for explanations. Please, let me use your car and I promise it will be returned to you as soon as possible."

Almost as if she were in a trance, she reached into her apron pocket and pulled out a set of keys. "I'm going to get fired," she said miserably. "It's the blue pickup in the employees' parking lot."

"Thanks." Nick released her and raced toward the door, his only thought to get to Alyssa.

By the time he got to the pickup, he was panting with pain and cursing the fact that he no longer had his gun. A wave of nausea rolled in his stomach, but he ignored it as he started the engine of the truck.

It was possible Murphy knew nothing about Alyssa, had no idea the depth of Nick's feelings for her. Please, let that be the case, he prayed.

But all he could think about was the fact that without Virginia in the bed-and-breakfast, without his presence there, Alyssa was alone...and vulnerable and had no idea that Nick's past had converged into his present and might intersect with her life.

He drove like a bat out of hell, his mind whirling. He hadn't had a chance to warn her about Murphy, and he hadn't had a chance to tell her that he hadn't meant the hurtful words he'd said to her in Ruby's.

It would take a very long time for him to forget the haunting pain that had darkened her eyes as he'd spoken to her in the café. Even though he knew his words had cut her to the quick, she'd responded with dignity, walking out of the café with her back straight and her head held high.

Let her be peacefully sleeping, he prayed. Let Murphy be resting beneath some rock far, far away from Alyssa. Nick couldn't lose her. He wouldn't lose her.

The closer he got to the bed-and-breakfast, the more strength he gained. It was strength borne in rage. Although he didn't want to remember that night three years ago in a motel room, memories of Dorrie and her death flashed through his head, whipping his rage to a fever pitch.

He'd loved Dorrie...and he loved Alyssa. And he was not going to allow Murphy to take her from him. He would do whatever it took to keep her safe.

If that meant staying with her every minute of every day, he'd do it. If that meant returning to Tulsa and never contacting her again, he'd do that, as well. Whatever it took to keep Murphy away from her.

He parked in the back parking lot, sucking air through his clenched teeth as he got out of the truck. Dammit. He didn't have keys.

He didn't want to bang on the door or call attention to himself. If Alyssa was asleep, then he would take guard outside her door for the remainder of the night. If Murphy was inside, he didn't want to push the man to do something deadly.

Knowing he couldn't get into the back door and the front door would be locked, as well, Nick sought an entrance through a window.

He found a window that opened easily into the dining room and he climbed through despite the pain that stabbed his back. Adrenaline pumped, and even though the rain had cooled the night, a trickle of sweat trailed down the side of his face.

Once inside he stood still and listened.

Nothing. No screams…no cries…no noise or movement to indicate anyone was in the house. The absence of sound should have made him relax, but it didn't. Murphy had killed Dorrie in a motel room with people staying in the rooms on either side. None of those people had heard a sound.

The only sound he could hear was the faint hum of the air conditioner and the rhythmic banging of his own heartbeat.

He felt naked without his gun, knew that if Murphy was here he needed a weapon. He crept into the kitchen aided by a small night-light that burned in a socket in that room. A block of wood on the island contained knives in all sizes…paring knives, steak knives and several butcher-size ones.

Nick pulled one of them out of the block. He'd watched Alyssa slice ham effortlessly with the knife and knew it would make a viable weapon if necessary.

Hopefully, it wouldn't be necessary. Hopefully, Alyssa was sleeping peacefully in her bed. He crept to the door that led into her private quarters. It was closed, as he'd expected it to be.

If it was locked, then he would have no other choice but to find another way in. But maybe with the trauma of the night's events, and knowing she was in the house alone, she hadn't locked the door.

With the knife firmly clenched in his right hand, he gripped the doorknob in his left and sighed in relief as it turned easily in his hand.

It opened soundlessly.

From his vantage point in the doorway he could see the open door of her bedroom…could see the man crouched on the bed…and he lost conscious thought…gave himself to the rage that had simmered in him for three long years.

He was unaware of making a sound as he lunged for the bedroom, but he must have roared. The man on the bed turned his head, his face radiating stunned surprise just before Nick threw himself at him.

Nick was vaguely aware of Alyssa as he and Murphy tumbled to the floor next to the bed. A piece of duct tape covered her mouth, and her wrists and ankles were tied to the bedposts. Although her eyes were wide open, her pretty beige dress was splashed with bright red blood.

Nick saw red as he and Murphy fell to the floor, then scrambled to their feet and faced each other.

"Agent Mead," Murphy said. "I'm afraid you've come at a bad time. I was just getting to know your lady friend here."

Nick backed the man up with a jab of his butcher knife, maneuvering so that he was between Murphy and Alyssa. "It's over, you bastard," he said.

Someplace in the back of Nick's mind, the specter of Murphy had become bigger than life. The man had taken on the proportions of a monster. But it was no monster who faced Nick with his own knife in hand.

The man who called himself Murphy was a small man with petite, almost feminine features and a fox-like cunning in his blue eyes. Nick had never seen him before in his life.

"It's not over," he said. "Not until you join your first wife in death. You were a naughty boy, Nick, saying mean things about me to the press. Naughty boys pay."

He slashed his knife at Nick, forcing Nick to jump back to avoid the deadly sharp steel of the blade. Nick was bigger, stronger, but Murphy was fast. Nick never saw the flash of the blade that flayed the forearm of his knifeless hand.

"First blood," Murphy nearly crowed in glee.

Nick kicked. It was a move Murphy obviously hadn't expected. Nick's foot connected with Murphy's hand and his knife flew through the air.

Nick charged. With his head lowered, he hit Murphy's midsection, heard the air whoosh out of the man as they both hit the floor.

Nick knew he'd ripped open whatever stitches had

been sewn into his back. He felt the warm flow of blood down his back, but it didn't stop him.

He crawled on top of Murphy, pinning him to the floor with his knife at his neck. "It's not important who draws the first blood, the winner is whoever draws the last blood."

He wanted to swipe the knife across Murphy's neck, steal his life as Murphy had stolen Dorrie's, as he'd intended to steal Alyssa's. His hand trembled with the need to seek vengeance and Murphy must have seen his desire in his eyes.

"Do it," Murphy hissed. "Go ahead, do it. Or are you a coward?"

How he wanted to. But someplace beneath the rage, he knew that in doing so he would be the same kind of monster as Murphy.

Instead, he used the tip of the knife to nick the skin, drawing a pinpoint of blood to the surface. "That would be too easy," he said. At the same time he heard the sound of a siren in the distance and knew Nurse Marianne had probably called the police.

Nick threw his own knife out of reach and instead used his hands to pin Murphy's arms over his head on the floor. Nick looked up at Alyssa. Tears flowed from her eyes and she nodded her head, as if to let him know she was okay.

But she wasn't okay. There was blood on the front of her dress and Nick had no idea what had transpired in this room before he'd arrived.

"Open up!" Glen Cleberg's voice sounded from

the front door. "Alyssa...Nick! Are you in there?"
He banged on the door.

"In here," Nick yelled. He wasn't about to get off
Murphy to open the door for the authorities. They
could break the door down if necessary, but Nick
wasn't about to release his hold on his nemesis.

He heard the crash of glass and knew they'd broken
the glass pane next to the front door and would be
inside within seconds. It was a good thing, because
with each beat of his heart Nick was losing blood and
strength.

"We've got him, Nick." Glen Cleberg strode into
the room and touched Nick on the arm. "You can let
him go now. We've got him."

Nick did. He rose from the floor where he'd had
Murphy pinned, and flew to Alyssa on the bed. With
as much tenderness as possible, he pulled the duct
tape from her mouth as officers worked on either side
of the bed to untie her wrists and ankles.

"She's bleeding," Nick cried out. "She needs
medical attention."

"I'm all right," she said. She threw her newly
freed arms around his neck and began to sob.

Until this moment he hadn't allowed himself to feel
his fear for her, but now it ripped through him.
Sharp...clawing, like a beast inside of him, his fear
consumed him as he held tight to her.

How close he'd come to losing her. It terrified him.
He would have clung to her all night long, but he
knew he was in trouble.

His vision began to blur and he felt the darkness

that he'd crawled out of only an hour before begin to sweep over him once again.

He fought it, wanting to hang on to her, to comfort her, but although he had been stronger than Murphy, he wasn't stronger than the invading weakness of his own body.

"Nick!" He heard Alyssa's cry as he slid into the darkness and knew nothing more.

Dawn had streaked the eastern sky an hour before as Alyssa stood at Nick's hospital-room window. She'd watched the sun peek over the horizon, then climb out of bed at full strength to promise another hot day.

She glanced at Nick, who was sleeping, then looked out the window once again. She had ridden in the ambulance that had brought him to the hospital and had only left his side when the doctor had re-stitched the wound in his back, stitched up his fore-arm and gotten him hooked back up to an IV.

The horror of the night had slowly begun to pass. Her wound, a nick of Murphy's knife on her chest, had been cleaned and bandaged, she'd showered to wash away his touch and was dressed in a pair of shorts and a T-shirt that one of the nurses had offered her.

"Hell of a night."

She turned from the window to see him smiling, that sexy, beautiful smile that twisted her insides in a way no other smile had ever done.

"You should be exhausted, Agent Mead," she said

as she moved from the window to sit in the chair next to his bed. "It isn't every night a man catches not one but two serial killers."

"Murphy?" he asked.

"Is in jail. I told Chief Cleberg about your wife and the other cases in Chicago. Murphy isn't going anywhere."

Nick's hand reached for hers and she welcomed the warmth of his fingers curling around hers. "Alyssa…about last night in the café. I didn't mean what I said to you."

"It's all right," she assured him. "I know you were trying to draw out Virginia."

"No, that was just an added benefit to my little show." He pressed a button to raise the head of his bed, a slight grimace sweeping over his features. "I staged that little scene in the café for Murphy's benefit. It was a stupid idea, but I needed to distance you from me as fast as possible. It was the only thing I could think of to do."

His hand squeezed hers. "Are you all right? Did he hurt you?"

She could see the torment in his eyes as he held her gaze intently. She knew what he was asking and she quickly shook her head. "No, he scared me terribly and he pricked my chest with his knife point, but he didn't really hurt me. He didn't touch me."

Nick closed his eyes, as if his relief was too much to bear. "I brought him to you." His near whisper held enough guilt, enough remorse, to last an eternity.

Alyssa leaned over him and placed her free hand

on his heart. "And then you saved me from him," she said softly. "And now it's all over...my vision, the killings, it's all over, Nick."

His eyes opened and he visibly relaxed. "Yes, it's all over. I'm free of Murphy and Cherokee Corners is free of Virginia and you're free of the vision that has been haunting you for so long."

He withdrew his hand from hers and instead raised it to lightly stroke down the side of her face. "Unfortunately, I'm not free of you." He dropped his hand and once again closed his eyes.

Alyssa sat motionless waiting for him to continue. She began to think he'd fallen back asleep, when his eyes opened once again. "I have no right to ask this of you...not after what I put you through last night, but I want you to come with me when I leave here. I love you, Alyssa, and I can't imagine spending the rest of my life without you."

The last thing Alyssa had been expecting were the words that came out of his mouth. They brought to her an incredible joy, but the joy was short-lived.

She knew Nick was being pumped full of antibiotics and pain medication. They had both been through a horrible night and emotions were closer to the surface than usual.

Alyssa still felt the lingering ugliness of her moments with Murphy. The darkness of her vision hadn't quite receded. Now wasn't the time to speak of love. "Nick..." She wasn't sure what she was going to say and was grateful when he held up a hand to still her.

"Don't answer me now," he said. "Take some time and think about it. I love you, Alyssa, and I want to spend the rest of my life with you, but you know what I do for a living and you have to decide if you can live with that."

It was obvious he was growing tired and Alyssa knew what he needed was to sleep…and she needed to think, to process everything that had happened in such a short space of time.

"Go home, sweetheart," Nick said softly. "Go home and sleep, go home and plan what you want your future to be." His eyes drifted closed and she knew the pain medicine had put him to sleep.

She stood for a long moment watching him and tears pressed hot against her eyelids. He loved her. He wanted to spend the rest of his life with her.

You will live your life alone, my little one. Her grandmother's words echoed in her head as she was driven home by Jason Sheller for the second time in the last twenty-four hours.

"We've got to stop meeting like this," Jason said as he pulled out of the hospital parking lot.

"Trust me, there's nothing I'd like more," she replied. She leaned her head back, closed her eyes and drew a deep breath. Fragments of pictures played in her mind… Virginia stabbing Nick in the park… Murphy promising her a painful death… Nick's confession of love.

It was too much…all of it was too much, and she was too tired to make sense of it all. He loves me. Her heart jumped with the sheer magic of those words, but underlying the joy was the thought of her grandmother's words.

You will live your life alone, my little one.

Tears once again sprang to her eyes. He loved her and he wanted to build a future with her, spend his life loving her, but she was afraid to ignore the vision her grandmother had seen for her.

She was afraid that Nick would only love her temporarily, then he'd grow tired of her visions, her blackouts, her craziness, and he'd leave and once again she'd be alone. Only this time she'd have no bed-and-breakfast, no temporary guests, nothing to assuage the emptiness that would be left behind.

Not having Nick's love at all would be far easier than having it temporarily. She couldn't stand the thought of building a life with Nick for days... weeks...months, then only to have it all fall apart.

Better to live her life alone...better to heed the vision that her grandmother had shared with her.

"You want me to call somebody for you?" Jason offered when he pulled up in front of the bed-and-breakfast.

"No, it's too early to bother anyone," she replied. "I'll be fine." She didn't want to see anyone right now, not with her heart so heavy.

She was only grateful she managed to get up the stairs and to the bed in the blue bedroom where she and Nick had loved before the tears truly began to fall.

Chapter 16

"Looks like a flower shop in here." Glen Cleberg leaned closer to read the card of a particularly large arrangement that had been delivered to Nick's hospital room.

"Yeah, they started arriving yesterday and haven't stopped." Nick sat on the side of the hospital bed to put on his shoes.

"The town is grateful to you, Nick." Glen shoved his hands in his pockets, a frown raking across his broad forehead. "We should have had Virginia a month ago. We should have checked her background more closely immediately after Greg's murder."

Nick stood from the bed. "What have you found out about her?" he asked curiously.

"It would appear that our Mrs. Maxwell was married before and that husband died under suspicious circumstances. She got a hefty insurance-policy pay-off, spent it, then when she was broke hooked up with Greg. We're also checking out the possibility of another husband before that one.''

''Sounds like what you have here is a genuine black widow. When you get all the information on her, I hope you'll send it to me at the Tulsa office.'' The woman had fooled them all with her waiflike helplessness and easy tears. She might have killed her husbands for money, but she'd continued to kill because she liked it. She liked the feeling of control it gave her.

''Of course. So, I suppose you'll be leaving here soon?''

''Probably sometime this afternoon.'' A wave of depression swept over Nick as he thought of leaving Cherokee Corners and Alyssa behind.

Glen's frown deepened. ''Are you sure you're fit to drive?''

''I'm fine. My shoulder and arm will heal nicely thanks to the good work of the doctor.'' Unfortunately, his heart hadn't fared as well.

''I've already heard from the authorities in both Chicago and Tulsa. It seems Murphy is a popular man…they both want him badly.''

Nick felt a peaceful satisfaction as he thought of the man who had killed so many women, including Dorrie. By the time he was convicted and sentenced for all his crimes, Murphy would die in prison.

''You got a ride out of here?'' Glen asked.

Nick nodded. ''Bud is coming to pick me up and take me back to the bed-and-breakfast.''

''Sure you don't want to stick around town for another day or two? The fall festival starts tomorrow. Things will be hopping out at the cultural center.''

''Thanks, but my work here is done and it's time for me to get back to my life in Tulsa.''

''I can't tell you how much we appreciate your help.'' Glen held out his hand to Nick. ''You're a good cop, Agent Mead, and one hell of a nice guy.''

Nick gripped the chief's hand in a firm shake. ''And you have a fine force here and a beautiful town.''

As their hands dropped back to their sides, Bud entered the hospital room. ''All set?'' he asked.

Nick nodded, then turned back to Chief Cleberg. ''Thanks for all your hospitality while we've been here.''

''I speak for the whole town when I tell you that we appreciate what you and your team accomplished. Men will be able to sleep peacefully once again.''

Minutes later Nick sat in Bud's passenger seat as Bud drove him to the Redbud. The two men made small talk, but Nick's mind was filled with thoughts of Alyssa.

She wasn't going to go with him to Tulsa. Even though she hadn't actually rejected his proposal, he knew the answer by the fact that for the past twenty-four hours he'd heard nothing from her.

A woman who was in love with a man and planned

to spend the rest of her life with him didn't allow him
to languish alone in a hospital room.

He'd known she was going to tell him no the moment he'd asked her to share his life. There had been
a flicker of joy in her eyes, followed by a shadowed
darkness that had ripped his heart into pieces. He'd
seen her answer in that darkness and knew he'd be
returning to Tulsa and a solitary life.

Bud pulled up along the curb in front of the bed-
and-breakfast. "You sure you're all right to make the
drive back home alone?" he asked.

"I'm fine," Nick assured him. "It isn't that long
a drive back."

"Then I guess we'll see you later," Bud said as
Nick got out of the car. "Drive safely."

"You guys do the same."

Nick stood at the curb and watched as Bud pulled
away, then he turned and faced the bed-and-breakfast.
It was over. The murders had been solved and his
time here in Cherokee Corners, his time here with
Alyssa, was over.

As crazy as it sounded, this seemed to hurt even
more than losing Dorrie. Dorrie had been stolen from
him by a madman. Alyssa was making the choice not
to be with him and that hurt more than anything Nick
had ever experienced.

He drew a deep breath and walked up the sidewalk
to the front door. As he walked, he glanced at his
wristwatch. It was just after eleven. He could pack up
and be on the road back to Tulsa by noon.

She met him at the door and the sight of her filled

him with an ache that rivaled the throbbing pain of his shoulder wound. "Nick." His very name from her lips sounded as if it was filled with her pain. She started to reach up to grasp the ends of her hair, letting him know she was unsettled...nervous.

He didn't want to make her nervous. He knew you couldn't get blood out of a turnip, nor could you make a woman love you enough to give up everything she knew to build a new kind of life.

"I'm just here to pack up my things and check out. I'm driving back to Tulsa today," he said. He headed for the stairs, wanting to make it as easy as possible for her...for him. Best to just get it over with and get out of here.

The bedroom brought a new wave of heartbreak for him as he looked at the bed where he and Alyssa had made love, had shared secrets, had held each other while stormy forces raged around them.

As he packed his clothes into the suitcase he'd brought with him when he'd first arrived, he told himself that he couldn't blame her for not accepting his proposal. With her visions, her life was filled with enough chaos. Marrying a criminal profiler who specialized in serial killers would only add more chaos to her life and mind.

It took a little longer to pack up the files he had and his laptop. When he was finished packing, he carried his things down the stairs and found Alyssa in the living room of her private quarters.

When Alyssa saw him she held out an invoice she'd apparently prepared while he'd been packing.

She didn't meet his gaze and she wore a look of miserable pain on her face.

He took the invoice from her, then drew a finger down the side of her face. She closed her eyes, as if his very touch only deepened her pain. When she opened her eyes and looked at him, her eyes swam with tears.

"Don't," he said softly, unable to stand her pain. "It's all right, baby. As much as I'd love to make you love me enough to want to marry me, I know I can't."

She stepped back from him, away from his touch. "Oh, Nick…it's not about loving you enough. I can't imagine loving anyone as much as I love you."

Nick stared at her in confusion. "Then what is it? What's keeping you from marrying me, from spending your life with me? Is it this place? Do you not want to leave here?"

She shook her head. He watched as she walked across the small room to the bookcase that held the array of baskets. She picked one up in her hands as tears trekked down her cheeks.

"I've told you before that my grandmother had visions like me. She was a wisewoman who tried to teach me everything she could about my visions and what I'd need to survive the darkness of the sight." She worried the basket in both her hands. "But one of the things she told me was of her vision of my life, and that vision was that I would always live alone, be alone."

He took the basket from her and placed it back on

the shelf, then placed his hands on her shoulders. "And you believe your grandmother's vision for your future over the one you must see in my eyes? Your grandmother had the sight and wasn't alone. She had a daughter and she had you."

She refused to meet his gaze and instead once again stepped away from him. Still, hope rose inside him as he realized love wasn't the problem. She loved him.

It was the vision of a dead woman that was stopping her from committing to him.

"Alyssa...you had a vision of me dying beneath a gnarled tree. We changed the ending of that vision. Just because your grandmother saw your life one way doesn't mean that it's the way it has to be."

"You don't understand," she said softly, still not meeting his gaze. "I can't do this, Nick. My place is here, my life is here...alone." There was a finality to her words that sounded a death knell inside him.

"With your temporary boarders that keep you from ever having to emotionally invest in anyone." He picked up his suitcase and briefcase. "In the time I've been here, I had come to believe that you were the bravest woman I've ever met. Now I see the truth, that you have more than a little bit of coward inside you."

Finally she looked at him, her expression radiating surprise. "I'm not a coward," she replied.

There was no point in continuing the conversation. He couldn't stand to be in this room, seeing the tears in her eyes, knowing they weren't going to share a future together. "I've got to go," he finally said. "I want to stop over at Ruby's and say goodbye before leaving town."

He gazed at her another long moment. "This isn't your grandmother's vision coming true, this is you choosing to make it so. You're living a self-fulfilling prophecy that will keep you alone."

As he turned and left her quarters, he prayed that she would stop him, that she would cry out his name and throw herself into his arms. He wanted her to tell him that she knew their love for each other was strong enough to change a vision that didn't speak of happiness and commitment and love forever more.

But she did none of those things and he walked out of the back door without being stopped. He was leaving Cherokee Corners with a stab injury in his back and a deep laceration in his arm, but neither could compare with the utter shattering of his heart.

For a long moment after he'd gone, Alyssa stood in the center of her living room and fought the heartbreak that ripped through her. She'd done the right thing...hadn't she?

She sank down on the sofa, wondering why, if she'd done the right thing, did she felt so sick inside, so filled with a kind of despair she'd never known before.

She had spent the last twenty-four hours fighting with herself, her heart telling her to take a chance on happiness and love, and her head warning her that to do so would only create more pain. Her head had won the battle, but now it was her heart paying the price, breaking into a million agonizing pieces.

"You're my happy, sane place." That's what he'd said to her, and as she'd walked through the darkness of her frightening visions, he had been hers.

"If this man, this Nick, fulfills you as a woman, then trust what's in your heart, not whatever visions might be in your head." That had been the advice from her aunt Rita.

Was she a coward? Was she afraid to take a chance and defy the vision her grandmother had had of her life? Was it as Nick had said, was she self-fulfilling a prophecy that didn't have to be?

Panic welled up inside her as she realized she'd just made the biggest mistake of her life. She sprang up from the sofa and ran out the door.

Outside, the sun was hot as she raced straight ahead, through the park to the other side of the square. The last time she'd run through here she'd been running away from Nick. This time she was running to him and all that he had to offer.

Please, don't let me be too late, she prayed as she ran. Her heart jumped as she saw his car parked outside the café. He was still here.

The place was jumping with an unusually large lunch crowd. Frantically, she scanned the crowd looking for Nick. She saw Ruby at the back of the restaurant and there was Nick, seated at a small table talking to the big, blond woman.

"Nick!" Alyssa cried out his name, unmindful of the stares of the diners around her.

He looked up and his brilliant blue gaze met hers. He must have seen the love spilling from her eyes, curving her lips upward. He had to have seen the frantic need that drove her into the café and to him.

He rose and started toward her. She didn't wait for him to come to her, but rather met him halfway. "Yes," she said breathlessly. "Yes, I want to marry you. Yes, I want to spend my life with you."

He grabbed her in his arms and pulled her tight against his chest. "Are you sure?" he whispered fervently. "Are you positive?"

"I've never been so sure of anything in my entire life." She barely got the words out of her mouth before his lips came crashing down on hers.

As he kissed her she was vaguely aware of clapping and hooting from the people around them. Tears once again burned in her eyes, but this time they were tears of happiness.

When the kiss ended, she looked into his eyes and her heart nearly burst from her chest in joy. "I have a vision," she said. "I see us living together for the rest of our lives, loving each other and having a family."

He framed her face with his hands, those beautiful blue eyes of his seeming to see inside her soul. "That's not a vision, my love, that's my promise to you."

Alyssa looked at Ruby, who stood nearby, her broad face beaming with a smile. "You still want to make an offer on my place?"

"Hell, yes," Ruby exclaimed and rubbed her hands together in obvious glee.

"Don't think you're going to get a bargain just because we're in love," Nick warned her.

She threw back her head and cackled. "I knew you were trouble the first day I saw you, handsome," she exclaimed.

"And I knew you were dangerous to me the first time I saw you," Alyssa said to Nick.

Nick took her by the arm and led her outside the café, away from the audience of the other people. When they were out in the bright sunshine, he once again took her in his arms.

"It will take me a while to settle things here before I can go to Tulsa," she said.

"It's not so far that I can't drive back and forth several times a week until you get free," he replied.

"I almost let you go," she said softly. "I almost let you walk out of my life."

He grinned, that beautiful, sexy grin that sent rivulets of heat flooding through her. "I wasn't gone yet. I'm not sure I could have made it out of town without trying one more time to convince you that we belong together."

"Forever," she said.

His eyes glowed with love. He was her happy, sane place, and as his lips once again sought hers in a fiery kiss Alyssa knew she would never, ever be alone again.

* * * * *

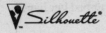

INTIMATE MOMENTS™

From reader favorite
SARA ORWIG

Bring on the Night

(Silhouette Intimate Moments, #1298)

With a ranch in Stallion Pass, Jonah Whitewolf
inherited a mysterious danger—a threatening
enemy with a vendetta against him. When he
runs into his ex-wife, Kate Valentini, in town,
he comes face-to-face with the secret she's kept—
the son he never knew. With the truth revealed,
Jonah must put his life in peril to protect his
ranch and his family from jeopardy. But can he
face the greatest risk of all and give himself up
to love a second time around?

STALLION PASS:
TEXAS KNIGHTS

*Where the only cure for those hot and sultry
Lone Star Days are some sexy-as-all-get-out
Texas Knights!*

Available June 2004 at your favorite retail outlet.

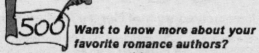

Silhouette®

INTIMATE MOMENTS™

A new generation begins
the search for truth in...

A Cry in the Dark

(Silhouette Intimate Moments #1299)

by Jenna Mills

No one is alone....

Danielle Caldwell had left home to make a new life
for her young son. Then Alex's kidnapping rocked her
carefully ordered world. Warned not to call for help,
Dani felt her terror threatening to overwhelm her
senses—until tough FBI agent Liam Brooks arrived on
her doorstep, intent on helping her find Alex. Their
clandestine investigation led to a powerful attraction
and the healing of old wounds—and the discovery
of a conspiracy that could unlock the secrets of
Dani's troubled past.

The first book in the new continuity

FAMILY
SECRETS
THE NEXT GENERATION

Available June 2004 at your favorite retail outlet.

1923
980
―――
943

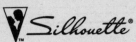

COMING NEXT MONTH